EVERY SECRET LEADS

SECRETS *of the* MANOR

Kate's Story, 1914

ADELE

Simon Spotlight
New York London Toronto Sydney New Delhi

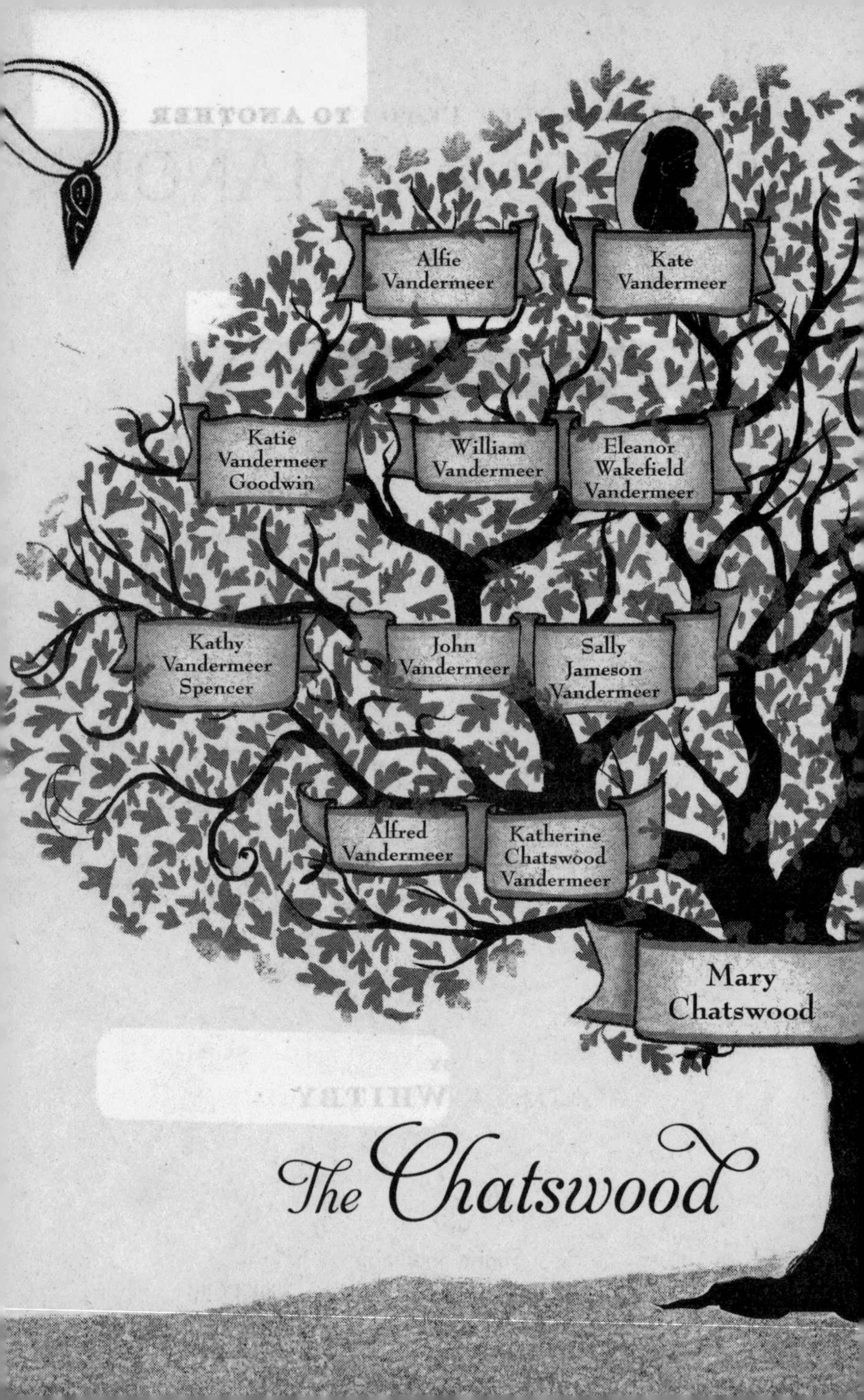
Alfie Vandermeer
Kate Vandermeer
Katie Vandermeer Goodwin
William Vandermeer
Eleanor Wakefield Vandermeer
Kathy Vandermeer Spencer
John Vandermeer
Sally Jameson Vandermeer
Alfred Vandermeer
Katherine Chatswood Vandermeer
Mary Chatswood
The Chatswood

Find a family tree, character histories, excerpts,
and more at SecretsoftheManor.com

replied, her grin widening. "Something tells me you were whispering and giggling about your party! Am I right?"

Katherine and I nodded. "We're going over the guest list with Papa and Mrs. Cosgrove after breakfast this morning," I added.

"I've a list of questions for you from Mrs. Fields and Mrs. Cosgrove," Essie replied, digging through the pockets of her apron until she found a small piece of paper. "We can go through some of them while I get you girls dressed and ready for the day. Beginning with what kinds of flowers you'd like."

"Blue hydrangeas," Katherine said.

"Red roses," I announced at the same time.

Then we laughed. Katherine's favorite color was blue, and mine was red. Of course we each wanted the flowers to be in our own favorite color.

Essie laughed along with us as she opened the doors to my armoire. She was used to us saying opposite things. It happened almost as often as we said exactly the same thing! Essie liked to say that she never knew what to expect from us. I figured that made us exciting to be around!

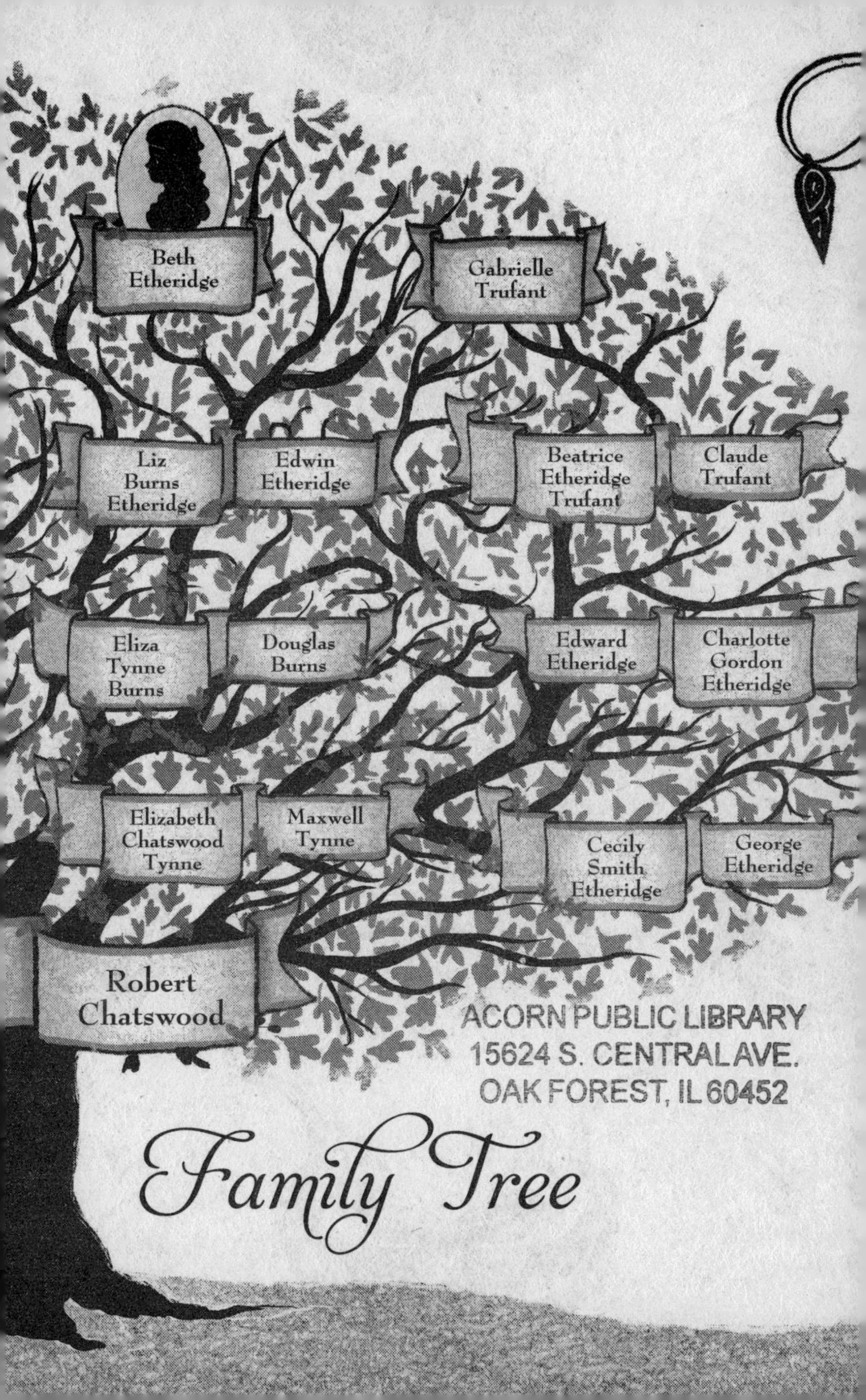
Beth Etheridge
Gabrielle Trufant
Liz Burns Etheridge
Edwin Etheridge
Beatrice Etheridge Trufant
Claude Trufant
Eliza Tynne Burns
Douglas Burns
Edward Etheridge
Charlotte Gordon Etheridge
Elizabeth Chatswood Tynne
Maxwell Tynne
Cecily Smith Etheridge
George Etheridge
Robert Chatswood
Family Tree

This book is a work of fiction. Any references to historical events, real people, or real places are used fictitiously. Other names, characters, places, and events are products of the author's imagination, and any resemblance to actual events or places or persons, living or dead, is entirely coincidental.

SIMON SPOTLIGHT
An imprint of Simon & Schuster Children's Publishing Division
1230 Avenue of the Americas, New York, New York 10020
This Simon Spotlight edition June 2014
 For information about special discounts for bulk purchases, please contact Simon & Schuster Special Sales at 1-866-506-1949 or business@simonandschuster.com.
Designed by Laura Roode. The text of this book was set in Adobe Caslon Pro.
Manufactured in the United States of America 0514 OFF
2 4 6 8 10 9 7 5 3 1
ISBN 978-1-4814-0635-2 (hc)
ISBN 978-1-4814-0634-5 (pbk)
ISBN 978-1-4814-0636-9 (eBook)
Library of Congress Catalog Card Number 2013943811

"'Then, with quaking hand, her ladyship reached for the rusty key hanging on the wall—'"

"Kate."

My mother's voice wafted to us from the doorway. I dropped my book as my lady's maid, Nellie, leaped to her feet. *Rats*, I thought. If it wasn't bad enough that Nellie and I had been caught reading when I should've been getting ready, now I'd lost my place in *The Hidden History of Castle Claremont*. And just when we were *finally* about to learn Lady Marian's secret!

"I trust you're ready for the meeting," Mother said with a pointed look at my stocking feet.

"Yes, Mother," I said as Nellie and I reached for my shoes at the same time, cracking our heads together. "Ow! I mean, I'm nearly ready. Just look at my hair. Didn't Nellie work wonders with it?"

"Very stylish," Mother said as a smile flickered across her lips. She always tried to be stern when she caught me breaking the rules, but she could never completely stop her smiles.

Nellie curtsied quickly. "Thank you, ma'am. Will there be anything else?"

"No, Nellie. I'll escort Kate to the garden myself," Mother replied.

With another curtsy and a nod of her head, Nellie scurried from the room.

Mother fixed her eyes on me. "Kate," she repeated.

"I know. And I'm sorry. I was ready, really I was. I just had to put my shoes on!" My words tumbled out in a rush. "See, it's my fault—not Nellie's. She loves to read but never has time, so when she does my hair, I read aloud so we can both enjoy the story. So you see, she really didn't do anything wrong—"

"No one is blaming Nellie."

I stopped talking. Mother slipped her arm through mine as we walked into the hallway.

"Kate, sweetheart, you're almost twelve years old," Mother continued. "It's high time you started acting like a Vandermeer in all that you say and do."

"But I—"

"I appreciate Nellie's love of stories. And she is welcome to spend her day off curled up with a book. But you must set an example for her. After all, if you don't behave as you're supposed to, how will Nellie and the other servants understand what is expected of them?"

We had almost reached the door. Mother paused and held both my hands. "You're ready, Kate," she said. "That's why your great-grandmother and I have decided that you've earned the privilege of attending your first meeting of the Bridgeport Beautification Society today. Sooner than you think, you'll be taking your place in society beside us. I'm sure I don't have to remind you how important the next eight days are."

I grinned at Mother. As if I could forget! In just over a week, my twelfth birthday would arrive at last. I would finally receive the Katherine necklace, a precious family heirloom that had been passed down to every Katherine in my family since my great-grandmother had received it on her twelfth birthday many years ago. Her twin sister, Elizabeth, had received a necklace, too. Each one was shaped like half a golden heart, but that was where the similarities ended. Elizabeth's

necklace was set with shimmering blue sapphires, while Katherine's glittered with red rubies—the twins' favorite colors. The necklaces were as meaningful as they were beautiful, for they were the last gift that the twins' mother, Lady Mary Chatswood, my great-great-grandmother, had selected for the girls before she died.

I'd heard the stories for years: that Elizabeth and Katherine were inseparable from the moment they were born. And they looked so much alike that their mother was the only one who could truly tell them apart. But only one twin could marry the heir to their English estate and become the next lady of Chatswood Manor. After Elizabeth became engaged to Cousin Maxwell, Great-Grandmother Katherine married my great-grandfather Alfred Vandermeer, and he brought her back to his home in America. Not soon after, my great-grandfather founded Vandermeer Steel, and the Vandermeer fortune grew and grew, what with Vandermeer steel incorporated in nearly every building, bridge, and train track constructed from then until this very day. His success enabled him to make his family home on the cliffs overlooking the ocean even grander. Today, Vandermeer Manor has

seventy-five rooms, four separate wings, five floors, and eight gardens. For many people in our town, it is the largest building they've ever seen. But for me, it is home. And my cousin, Beth—great-granddaughter of the original Lady Elizabeth Chatswood—would arrive here in just five days! I was so excited to meet Beth at last that I could hardly think about anything else. We knew each other only through letters, but it was obvious that we had so much in common. Our birthdays were just one month apart, and as the first girls in our generation, we shared the privilege of being named after the original Elizabeth and Katherine. I love my Great-Grandmother Katherine more than words can say, and I am honored to be her namesake. And I knew that Beth felt the same way about her name, even though her great-grandmother Elizabeth had died before Beth was born.

"Make me proud today, Kate," Mother said to me as Emil, one of the footmen, stepped forward to open the doors to the garden. "Like you always do."

Instantly, I put on my best, brightest smile. It had seemed so vain to practice it in the mirror, but now I was glad that Mother had insisted. "When all eyes are

on you, you'll find it hard to smile naturally," she had told me. And she was right.

Mother and I walked down the cobblestone path to the shade garden on the north side of the house. It was edged by massive hydrangea and lilac shrubs, which formed the walls of a perfect outdoor room. Their crisp white flowers were startling against the dark green foliage. A large elm tree provided just enough shade that the ladies didn't need their parasols. They milled about in summery pastel gowns trimmed with lace, looking for all the world like the saltwater taffy display in Sloane's Sweets and Confections down by the seashore. Anton, Emil's cousin and another one of our footmen, offered them tall glasses of icy lemonade. Mr. Taylor, our butler, stood against the gate, overseeing every aspect of the event.

Aunt Katie seemed relieved to see us as we entered the shade garden; it must have been exhausting to entertain the ladies of the Bridgeport Beautification Society by herself. I realized right away that Great-Grandmother Katherine was missing.

"My dear Eleanor," Aunt Katie said as she embraced Mother.

"Where is she?" Mother asked in a low voice.

"I'm afraid that Grandmother Katherine sends her deepest regrets," Aunt Katie said with a tight smile. "She had pressing business to attend for the Library Committee."

Mother nodded brusquely. "And I suppose she required Kathy's assistance?"

"Of course," Aunt Katie replied as she and Mother exchanged a knowing look.

Before I could wonder what that look meant about where my great-aunt Kathy and my great-grandmother Katherine really were, Mrs. Randolph, the president of the Bridgeport Beautification Society, bustled over to us. She wore a gown of pale gray silk and an enormous, wide-brimmed hat trimmed with trailing plumes, making her look more like a pigeon than a person. Still, I remembered my best manners and smiled pleasantly.

"How lovely you all look! And how lovely the day!" Mrs. Randolph cooed to my mother and Aunt Katie. "If it's quite all right with you both, I'd like to call our meeting to order. We've so much on the agenda; it will be a wonder if we cover it all!"

"I'm sure you'll be able to guide us to its conclusion,

Mrs. Randolph," Mother said sweetly. Then she and Aunt Katie sat at each end of the table, sending a signal to all the other ladies that they should be seated as well.

I slipped into the chair next to Mother with a quick glance over my shoulder. Our cook, Mrs. Hastings, had prepared the most delicious food for the meeting—cucumber sandwiches, berry tarts, madeleine cookies. I couldn't wait for Emil and Anton to fill my plate.

Mrs. Randolph held up her crystal glass and tapped it lightly with her fork. *Ting-ting-ting-ting.* "Ladies, as always, I thank you for your tireless commitment to the Bridgeport Beautification Society," she announced. "Mrs. Whitmore, would you please read the minutes from last week's meeting?"

As Mrs. Whitmore began to speak, my mind started to wander. It's not that I wasn't interested in what she had to say. But I could hardly focus on a discussion of paint colors for the gazebo in Town Square when my cousin Beth was, at this very moment, journeying to the United States! It was still hard to believe that Beth was on her way—especially since her parents had always said that Beth wouldn't be allowed to travel

all the way to America until she was at least fourteen years old. But the astonishing events surrounding Beth's twelfth birthday last month had changed their minds. Beth's beloved lady's maid, Shannon, was dismissed after Beth's cousin Gabby's missing heirloom locket was found in Shannon's laundry basket. Beth had set out to prove Shannon's innocence, and because of her determination to discover the truth, Beth figured out what really happened and cleared Shannon's good name. Beth's parents were so impressed that they booked her passage to visit her American relatives. And as luck would have it, Beth—wearing the Elizabeth necklace—would be here for my birthday, when I would receive the Katherine necklace!

When Mrs. Whitmore finished reading the minutes, Emil appeared with the dessert cart. My mouth watered at the sight of all the tiny cakes, each one topped with a juicy strawberry.

"Now, our business today deals with applications to march in the Fourth of July parade," Mrs. Randolph said in a serious voice. "I needn't remind you all of how important this is. The entire town looks to us to safeguard the proud traditions of the parade. Mrs. Whitmore?"

Mrs. Whitmore rummaged through the papers before her. "First, we have an application from the Rose Appreciation Society. Their statement of purpose is to bring the beauty of roses to Bridgeport, and they propose a float decorated with the finest examples of the flower."

"Lovely," Mrs. Randolph said approvingly. "All in favor, say aye."

"Aye," chorused the women around the table.

Emil wheeled the dessert cart behind me. With silver tongs, he carefully placed the most beautiful cake on my plate. "For you, Miss Kate," he whispered.

"Thank you, Emil!" I whispered back.

"Next, we have an application from the Brass Band of Bridgeport," Mrs. Whitmore read. "They would like to play patriotic music as they march along the parade route."

Mrs. Randolph chuckled. "Why, it wouldn't be a parade without them," she declared. "All in favor?"

"Aye!" everyone replied.

"This application is from the Library Committee," Mrs. Whitmore continued. "Their purpose is to support the Bridgeport Lending Library, and they'd like

to dress as characters from great American literature for their float."

"A clever idea!" Mrs. Randolph said approvingly. "All in favor?"

"Aye!"

"Here we have an application from the Suffragette Sisterhood, Bridgeport Chapter," Mrs. Whitmore said. "Their purpose is to advocate for the women of Bridgeport and all women in the United States to gain the right to vote. They propose a float decorated with—"

"Absolutely not," Mrs. Randolph interrupted, her voice sounding like ice. "Next."

I sat straighter in my chair. Now *this* was unusual. Why was the Suffragette Sisterhood excluded? I waited for one of the members of the Bridgeport Beautification Society to speak.

But no one did.

Mrs. Whitmore slowly reached for another application. There were just seconds left to raise an objection—

"Excuse me, Mrs. Randolph," I said. My voice sounded small; I hardly recognized it. "Might I ask why?"

Mrs. Randolph blinked at me through her silver-framed spectacles. "Why what, my dear?"

"Why isn't the Suffragette Sisterhood welcome in the parade?"

"The Suffragette Sisterhood is not welcome in Bridgeport, let alone an honored spot in our Fourth of July parade!" Mrs. Randolph declared. "I shudder to think that anyone might believe that such a group of ragtag women—let's not mistake them for ladies—would represent us. They are a blight on our town's good name."

"How can that be?" I asked. "Surely women deserve the right to vote as much as men do." This was a topic that had often been discussed at our dinner table—and I knew for a fact that Mother, Aunt Katie, Great-Aunt Kathy, and Great-Grandmother Katherine all agreed with me. As did Father and even my unbearable little brother, Alfie!

Mrs. Randolph made a clucking sound in her throat. "Oh, my dear, you are so very young," she said with a condescending smile. "How confused you must be! Women don't need to vote. They need husbands who will make decisions that benefit them both."

"It seems to me that—" I began.

"My! Look at the time!" Mrs. Randolph exclaimed. "We are behind schedule! Mrs. Whitmore, please inform the suffragettes that we have no room for them in the parade. Now, which application is next?"

Crash!

We spun around to see Emil, shaking like a leaf, with Anton by his side. Emil's copper tray trembled on the cobblestones, surrounded by fallen cookies that peeked through the grass.

Mr. Taylor hurried over to them, squinting at the mess through his thick glasses. "What is the meaning of this?" Mr. Taylor demanded. It was clear that our butler's poor vision prevented him from seeing how upset Emil was.

"Our deepest apologies for the interruption," Anton said as he knelt to clean the mess. "We beg your pardon."

As Emil whispered frantically to Anton, Mrs. Randolph frowned at them. "I should like another cup of tea," she said pointedly.

Neither footman seemed to hear her.

"Emil, what's wrong?" I asked in concern.

He tried to speak, but shook his head instead.

"The Archduke Ferdinand has been murdered," Anton replied for his cousin. "Shot and killed in the streets of Sarajevo!"

Everyone at the table gasped.

"This will lead to war," Emil said quietly. "And my family is still in Europe—who will protect them?" He buried his face in his hands, as if he had lost all hope.

Mr. Taylor cleared his throat loudly, but there was sympathy in his eyes. "Anton, please take Emil inside so that he may compose himself."

Anton stiffened his shoulders before he bowed. "Of course, Mr. Taylor. Right away," he replied. Then, without further fuss, Anton and Emil disappeared into the house. Moments later, two more footmen appeared to finish cleaning the mess, while another brought a fresh tray of cookies. It was almost as if the accident had never happened.

"Do you really think it will come to war?" Mrs. Abernathy asked in a trembling voice, and I remembered that her husband served as a captain in the army.

"Now, Marilyn, I thought you had more sense than that." Mrs. Randolph clucked at her. "I, for one, don't seek out news of the world from servants."

"Funny," Mother said lightly. "If I wanted to know about the state of the world, our employees are among the first people I'd ask."

"Oh, Eleanor, you've always been soft-hearted," Mrs. Randolph conceded. Then she glanced at me. "Kate! You look as though you've seen a ghost! Poor dear. There is really nothing to worry about. Europe is very far away, you know. A war on those distant shores wouldn't affect us, not in the least."

I tried to smile. "Yes, Mrs. Randolph," I replied. "I'm sure you're right."

But I wasn't sure. It would be hard to forget the look on Emil's face, the fear in his voice, and his quiet warning that this would lead to war.

Two days later, Nellie and I were interrupted by a loud and incessant knocking at my door. We exchanged a wary glance. There was only one person at Vandermeer Manor who knocked like that: my younger brother, Alfie. Named after our great-grandfather Alfred, who had died nearly twenty years ago, Alfie swaggered through the halls of Vandermeer Manor like he already owned it.

"Come in," I said with a sigh.

"Morning, Kate," Alfie said as he loped into the room. "I hope I'm not interrupting you."

"You are."

"Aw, don't be like that—or I might reconsider the very special birthday present I'm planning for you," he replied. "What are you up to, anyway?"

I eyed my brother suspiciously. Alfie seemed

sincere. But was it just a trap?

"Nellie and I are choosing outfits for my birthday celebrations," I explained.

Alfie's green eyes sparkled with mischief. "That *is* important work," he said gravely. "Here. Let me help. I think this hat with this dress, and of course you'll need an extra pair of gloves at the party after you grab yourself a fistful of cake—"

"Alfie! Stop! You're making a mess of everything!" I cried as he tossed my best clothes and accessories around the room. But that only made him laugh harder. In fact, Alfie didn't stop until Nellie fell to her knees to start picking up his mess. Then, for just a moment, a flicker of guilt crossed his face. *Good*, I thought. *It's about time Alfie started acting his age.* Just because he was the baby of the family, Mother and Father spoiled him rotten—even though he was nine years old already.

Alfie cleared his throat. "Right. I, um, Mother wants to see you."

"Why?" I asked.

"How should I know?" Alfie shot back. "Are you coming? Or maybe you'd like me to tell her that you're too busy."

I sighed. "Nellie, I'll be back soon," I promised. "I'm sorry about the mess." I glared at Alfie, but when he didn't say anything, I waved my hands in front of his face to get his attention.

"Okay, okay," said Alfie. "Yes, Nellie, I'm sorry. Here. Let me help." To his credit, Alfie did look genuinely sorry as he reached down and scooped up big armfuls of silk and satin. Then he dropped my gowns in a tangled heap on the bed.

"Oh, leave it, Alfie," I said firmly as I pulled him out the door. "You're just making it worse."

I walked toward the staircase, but Alfie grabbed my arm. "Actually, Mother's on the East Veranda," he said. That awful twinkle was back in his eyes.

"All right," I said slowly. "I'll just go downstairs and take the other stairs to her."

"Really, Kate?" Alfie chided me in that infuriating way of his. "That's pretty far out of your way, don't you think? Wouldn't it be easier to stay upstairs? Of course, then you'd have to walk by the East Wing. But that shouldn't be a problem . . . right? After all, it's not like it's haunted. It's not like you're *afraid.*"

"Of course not," I said stiffly.

"This way," Alfie said.

Neither of us spoke as we walked through the halls. Vandermeer Manor was so large that we simply had no use for the small East Wing that extended out of the back of the house. But I'd heard what the housemaids whispered when they thought no one was listening.

"Poor Blythe Fontaine," Alfie said suddenly.

Oh, no, I thought, as dread settled in the pit of my stomach. Everyone in Bridgeport knew about Blythe Fontaine. Just the thought of her terrible fate could keep me up for hours in the dark of night. If Alfie ever realized how much I hated the tale, he'd never stop telling it.

"I asked Father to show me where Captain Evans proposed to Miss Fontaine," Alfie continued. "But he said he didn't know, since all that happened before Vandermeer Manor was even built."

"Are you excited about the parade?" I said, hoping to change the subject. But Alfie ignored me.

"I wonder if Miss Fontaine buried Captain Evans's fortune," he said. "After he was lost at sea. That's what I would do, so robbers couldn't steal it. But maybe she was so busy walking the cliffs that she forgot."

Despite myself, my skin started to crawl.

"You remember the story, right?" Alfie asked, giving me a sideways glance. "How Miss Fontaine wouldn't marry Captain Evens until he gave up the sea, so he set sail one last time, on the voyage of a lifetime—all the way around the world. Miss Fontaine waited for him, walking back and forth along the cliffs day after day . . . after day . . . after day. . . . Weeks passed, then months, then a year. She never stopped walking the cliffs, searching for him. It was the November rains that did her in. She caught pneumonia but kept walking . . . walking . . . walking . . . until the day she fell down and died . . . on this very spot . . . and her spirit never left. Vandermeer Manor was built around her ghost, and even today she paces the cliffs, searching for her lost love."

"But, Alfie, there's no such thing as—"

He grabbed my wrist so suddenly that I jumped. "Shhh!" Alfie hissed. "She can *hear* you!"

With a sinking feeling, I realized that we were standing right outside the entrance to the East Wing. There was a small door that had been painted to match the wall.

His fingers still wrapped around my wrist, Alfie pulled me toward the door. "Listen," he whispered.

"No," I replied. "There's nothing there. Nobody goes into the East Wing."

"Then why won't you listen at the door?" Alfie asked. "Unless you're . . . scared?"

"I am not."

A positively infuriating smile crept across Alfie's face. "Never mind, Kate," he said kindly—too kindly. "I didn't mean to frighten you. Quick, now, run along to Mother and put all these scary thoughts out of your head."

"I'm *not* scared!" I insisted. And to prove it, I stuck my ear against the door. Alfie was quiet and so was I; we were quiet as little mice. But try as I might, I heard nothing.

Then I caught it: tinny, metallic, the sound of something being dragged across the floor.

I leaped back so quickly that I stumbled over my own feet, landing in a graceless heap. Alfie doubled over, laughing like he was fit to burst. That's when I noticed the metal square in his hand and the scratched paint on the door frame. Suddenly, I understood everything: Alfie had scraped that piece of metal on the edge of the door to make the otherworldly sound carry through the wood.

"You're *rotten*," I yelled. "You're a *rotten rat*!"

"Your face!" Alfie howled. "You should've seen your face!"

I stormed off, leaving Alfie alone with his laughter. His guffaws followed me all the way to the East Veranda, where Mother was reading the morning mail while Aunt Katie and Great-Aunt Kathy worked on their embroidery.

As I stepped onto the bright veranda, I realized how foolish it was to be so frightened of Alfie's ghost story. The sun sparkling on the water made the ocean look like a sea of sapphires. Far in the distance, we could see swimmers in their bathing costumes bobbing on the waves. The blistering heat of summer had arrived, but you'd never know it from the fresh sea breeze that danced around Vandermeer Manor.

I waited for a pause in Great-Aunt Kathy and Aunt Katie's conversation before I spoke.

"Mother, you wanted to see me?" I asked.

"Kate, dear," Mother said as she glanced up. "There's a letter for you."

"For me?" I asked curiously. Beth's tiny, perfect handwriting stared up at me from the envelope. I

ripped it open eagerly; four small, foreign stamps fluttered to the ground. Beth always remembered my stamp collection and made sure to send me any unusual postage that came to Chatswood Manor.

25 June 1914

My Dearest Cousin Kate,

I ask you in advance to please excuse the haste with which I write to you. In three days, we depart for the ship—and less than a week after that, I will arrive in America! I confess that I am not a bit ready; Shannon and I have been working ourselves ragged in our attempts to decide what, exactly, she should pack for my extended stay with you this summer. It's not just choosing the gowns, of course, but so much more—which hats and which gloves and which shoes and which jewels, and on and on and on. . . . I count myself even more fortunate now to have received

the Elizabeth necklace for my birthday earlier this month, since it spares me the challenge of packing necklaces. I love my Elizabeth necklace so much, dear cousin. I am sure you'll feel the same way when the Katherine necklace becomes yours!

Last week, Cousin Gabby, Aunt Beatrice, and Uncle Claude returned to France. I was honestly sorry to see them go. After Gabby pretended that her heirloom locket had been stolen and stood by silently while poor Shannon was blamed, I thought I'd be glad to see her leave. But after the truth came out, Gabby behaved much more like the charming cousin I remembered.

It was very kind of you to ask about my favorite foods, but please don't trouble yourself on my account. I'm not so particular that I'd ask your cook to take extra pains for me. I am looking forward to trying American fare. Do you take

afternoon tea? I thought perhaps not, but Mother reminded me that Great-Great-Aunt Katherine may have kept the old traditions alive, even after she made her home in a new land. I must tell you that I am simply beside myself with anticipation when I think of meeting her at last. It has always saddened me that Great-Grandmother Elizabeth died before I was born. To meet her twin is an experience I have long desired.

And to meet you, sweet Kate, will be a dream come true!

I will end this now, as Shannon waits patiently to consult with me about which gown I should pack for your birthday party. I hope I will choose the right one, Kate. I wish I'd thought to ask you more about the current fashions in America. Oh, I'd hate to look foolish and—even worse—embarrass you. But I have a

feeling you would forgive me if I did.

With greatest affection and so much delightful anticipation,

I remain,

Your Cousin Beth

PS I promised myself that I would not write of it, as I didn't want to ruin the surprise, but I have found something that is most mysterious and unusual, and I have decided to bring it with me to America so that you may see it for yourself. Now that I have piqued your interest, Cousin, I will refrain from saying more. Don't be cross with me! I'll be by your side—with my secret surprise—as soon as the waves will carry me.

"Any news?" Mother asked as I returned the letter to its envelope.

"Beth is very excited to visit," I replied. "And she

answered the questions from my last letter. She wants to try American foods."

Mother looked at me thoughtfully for a moment. "I'll ring for Mrs. Taylor," she said. "This is a good opportunity for you to give her instruction, Kate."

"But what should I say?" I asked as Mother reached for the bellpull.

"Just tell her what you'd like to be served during Beth's stay," she advised.

In moments, the housekeeper joined us. "What can I do for you?" Mrs. Taylor asked Mother as she took a leather-bound notebook from her apron pocket.

"Mrs. Taylor, I was hoping you might share the latest information about the plans for Kate's birthday party."

"Of course, ma'am. The guest count stands at four hundred and thirty, including the family. The menu is confirmed, and Mrs. Hastings and I have placed orders for all the necessary ingredients. Mr. Gleason called yesterday with an idea for the decorations. In addition to the rose garlands you ordered, he proposed a beautiful seashell near every place setting, a little favor for each guest, in honor of this manor by the sea."

"That sounds lovely," Mother said. "What do you think, Kate?"

I started in surprise. Usually I did nothing more than listen quietly to Mrs. Taylor's reports. "Yes, I agree," I said.

"Mr. Gleason also sent final sketches for the ice sculptures—a dozen swans of various sizes, to be placed in several locations around the ballroom. I think you'll be pleased."

"Yes, I'm sure I will; Mr. Gleason does beautiful work," Mother said. "Thank you, Mrs. Taylor. That was a very helpful update. Now, Kate has received word from her cousin Beth, who as you know, will be arriving here on the third of July. Kate?"

Mother and Mrs. Taylor turned to me. I took a deep breath as I unfolded Beth's letter. "Mrs. Taylor, Beth writes that she doesn't require any special foods," I began. "She has, um, she has expressed an interest in trying American fare while she is here."

Mrs. Taylor's eyes twinkled. "American fare! Your cousin is an adventurous young lady. We will have no shortage of American fare for her, Miss Kate, I can assure you. Would you be interested in hearing some

of the menus we have planned?"

"Yes, Mrs. Taylor, that would be fine," I replied.

"On the Fourth of July, there will be a picnic luncheon in the gazebo, after the parade," Mrs. Taylor reported. "Cold fried chicken, biscuits, potato salad, deviled eggs, watermelon, and cherry pie. That evening, there will be a clambake on the cliff, accompanied by corn on the cob, a salad of green beans and tomatoes, and a layer cake."

I glanced at Mother, who nodded at me encouragingly.

"Beth loves chocolate," I said. "Perhaps the layer cake could be a chocolate one."

Mrs. Taylor made a note. "Of course, Miss Kate."

"Thank you. Finally," I said, "Beth wonders if we take afternoon tea. She asks if Great-Grandmother Katherine keeps any of the customs from home."

This brought about a gale of giggles from my aunts. "Dear child," Great-Aunt Kathy said. "The day my mother abandons afternoon tea is the day that pigs will soar on gossamer wings."

"If you'd like, Miss Kate, we can serve proper British tea often while Beth is here," Mrs. Taylor suggested. "That might ease any homesickness your cousin feels.

And Mr. Taylor assures me that Mrs. Hastings's scones taste as authentic as the ones he enjoyed as a boy."

"What a nice idea," I said.

"My pleasure, Miss Kate," she replied.

A long pause followed. I wasn't sure what to say next.

"Will there be anything else?" Mrs. Taylor finally asked.

I glanced at Mother, who shook her head. "No, thank you, Mrs. Taylor," I said.

Mrs. Taylor nodded before she left the room.

"Well done," Mother said as she patted my hand. "You spoke clearly and kindly while giving instructions to Mrs. Taylor."

"Thank you, Mother. May I be excused?"

"Yes, Kate. I'll see you at lunch."

By the time I returned to my room, Nellie had cleaned up Alfie's mess.

"Oh, Nellie, it looks so nice in here!" I exclaimed. "I'm sorry about Alfie. He's just horrid sometimes."

"Well, as my mother always said, boys will be boys," Nellie replied.

"That's just an excuse," I said. "He doesn't *have* to

act like such a—a—a miscreant. Why should you have to clean up the mess he made, for no reason?"

There was a look in Nellie's eyes that I couldn't quite read. "Everything all right with your mother, Kate?" she asked, changing the subject.

"Oh! Nellie, look at this!" I cried, remembering Beth's letter. "A letter from Beth!"

Nellie pounced on the letter as eagerly as I had. When she finished reading it, Nellie sighed happily. "To think that in just a few days, Lady Beth will be *here*, in this very room," she said. "I can't wait to meet her and hear her accent. I hope she'll tell us all about life in England. I can hardly believe that we'll have a highborn lady staying at Vandermeer Manor!"

"A highborn lady?" I repeated. "You sound like a character from a novel."

Nellie grinned. "I can't help myself," she admitted. "I'm so interested in everything about England. I was born there, you know. And my grandparents still live there—along with a whole slew of cousins I've never even met."

"I didn't know that," I said. "What brought you to the United States?"

"My mother and father were looking for a new life—one with more opportunities for them and, one day, for me. But they died of typhoid when I was sixteen years old. Now I'm the last one here."

I reached for Nellie's hand. "Oh, Nellie," I breathed. "I'm so sorry."

"You're kind, Miss Kate," she said. "I'm grateful for my English relatives, even if they are so far away. We write as much as we can, and they never let my birthday pass without a parcel full of surprises. Someday, I hope I'll have the chance to meet them all."

"I'm sure you will," I said.

Nellie and I exchanged a smile, but there was no mistaking the sadness in her eyes. To be half a world away from my family would be almost unbearable. For sweet Nellie's sake, I hoped she could see her family soon.

3

A few days later, my eyes snapped open before dawn. The long wait was almost over; Beth would arrive this afternoon! I leaped out of bed, too excited to spend another moment lying down. I was about to reach for the call button to summon Nellie to my room when my hand paused. It was still dark outside. The tiny clock ticking on my mantel read a quarter to five.

If Nellie's still asleep, it would be wrong to wake her, I decided. *Especially since I don't need anything besides a little company.*

I yanked the down comforter off my bed and dragged it across the room. Then I curled up in the window seat overlooking the ocean so that I could watch the sun rise. Faintly, I could hear the sound of the waves lapping onto the shore and the distant cry of a seagull. A heavy mist hung over the ocean, seeping all the way to the house, but I could see a smudge of pale light at the far edge of the horizon where the sun would soon rise.

Then, something caught my eye in the garden below. I squinted as I peered through the window, trying to get a better look. It almost looked like . . . no, that couldn't be right. . . . But it did; it really did. It looked like a woman, veiled in black from head to toe.

It's Blythe Fontaine's ghost! She's searching for the captain! I thought suddenly. *No. Of course not. That is just a story. It isn't real.*

The figure moved toward Vandermeer Manor, creeping through the silvery mist.

I was trembling all over; my mouth was so dry that I could barely swallow, but I couldn't tear my eyes away. I wanted to call out for help, but my voice was as paralyzed as the rest of me. Far away, over the ocean, the red sun began to rise, but the grayness of dawn hung heavily over the gardens. The figure kept walking toward the house. I watched her for as long as I could before I lost sight of her behind the hedges near the East Wing.

Moments later, the sun rose, spilling golden light over the ocean and the gardens. With such a cheerful

sun shining, it was hard to believe what I'd seen. *Had I fallen asleep? Did I merely dream of the ghostly figure?* I wondered—or perhaps I should say that I wished. Because I knew, without a doubt, that the black-clad figure was all too real.

That afternoon, Mother, Father, and I climbed into the back of the car. Our chauffeur, Hank, paused before he shut the door. "Miss Kate, you'll want to mind the door," he said as he gestured to my skirts, which were sticking out of the door.

"Sorry!" I exclaimed with a giggle as I pulled the lace-trimmed silk into the car. I was so excited to meet my cousin that I had turned into a scatterbrain!

Hank smiled at me as he tipped his cap. "Right, then," he said with just a hint of a lilting Irish accent. "Next stop, Providence Station. We'll be there well in time for the two-o'clock arrival from New York City."

"Thank you, Hank," Father said as he opened his newspaper. His forehead was grooved with deep furrows as he examined the front page. "Nasty business in Europe, Eleanor," he said to Mother. "There is already speculation of war."

"Goodness, I hope not," Mother said right away. "Surely it can be prevented."

Father stroked his beard with an absent look in his eyes. "It could've been," he replied. "Might be too late now. A pity. I'll be keeping a close eye on the situation. If the worst comes to pass, Vandermeer Steel will be poised to make a pretty penny."

Mother shuddered slightly. "A penny earned from warfare is not one worth earning," she said firmly.

By the time we reached the station, my parents had moved on to talking about the Fourth of July festivities instead of the possibility of war in Europe, but I confess I wasn't paying much attention to their conversation. The station was bustling with activity as people gathered to meet the oncoming train. I could hear the clattering of its wheels on the tracks and smell the thick, black smoke that poured from its locomotive. When the train itself finally appeared, my heart leaped. Somewhere, in one of those cars, sat my cousin!

The train's brakes squealed as it slowed to a stop. I was about to dash over to the tracks when Mother caught my arm. "We'll wait here, Kate," she said. "Hank will find them."

As if on cue, Hank stepped forward with a small sign reading ETHERIDGE in neatly printed letters. He walked past us and stood at the very edge of the platform. I stared eagerly at every person who climbed off the train, searching for a face that might belong to Beth. Would I recognize her the moment she stepped off the train? Would she look like me . . . or like a stranger?

"Here, sir! Over here!" a high-pitched voice called out. The young woman's strong Irish accent caught my attention—and Hank's—right away. As she started to take a tentative step down the stairs toward the platform, Hank reached out his hand to steady her. Before she exited the train, the woman turned to face someone behind her, someone who was still hidden in the shadows. But I knew right away who it was, and I couldn't wait any longer.

I broke away from my parents and ran to the edge of the platform as Hank helped Shannon and Beth out of the train. "Beth! Beth!" I shrieked. "It's me! It's Kate!"

"Cousin Kate!" she cried. Then we were a jumble, jumping and hugging and laughing, even crying.

"How was the train? Did you like New York? Did you stay in my room? I hope it was cool enough; the city gets so miserably hot in the summer. Did you enjoy the voyage? I've never been on a steamer before. Was it a smooth crossing, or did you pass through rough waters?"

As I paused to take a deep breath, Beth burst out laughing. After a moment, Hank and Shannon joined in, and so did I.

"Bumpy, yes, yes, certainly, yes, smooth enough!" Beth replied, all in a rush, and everyone laughed again. She reached out and squeezed my hand. "Oh, Kate! I can't believe I'm here!"

"I can't believe it, either," I replied. "We have so much planned, Beth. I think you're going to have the best time—"

"Kate!" Mother's voice carried across the platform. "Kate!"

I'd almost forgotten that my parents were waiting for us. "Come on. Mother and Father are dying to meet you too," I said as I brought Beth over to them. Mother's smile held the warmth of a hundred suns as she pulled Beth into an embrace.

"Welcome, Beth! We're so glad that you could visit!" she said. "How are you, my dear?"

"Very well, thank you, Mrs. Vandermeer," Beth said with a formal curtsy.

"Now, I suppose we're actually cousins, but you must call us aunt and uncle," Father said as he shook Beth's hand. "We'll have none of these formalities between family."

Beth smiled warmly and pulled Shannon forward. "And this is Shannon, my lady's maid," she said.

"Very good to meet you, Shannon," Mother said graciously. "Kate's maid, Nellie, is at the house. She'll take good care of you."

Father turned to Hank. "See about the luggage, will you, Hank?"

Hank touched the brim of his cap. "Certainly, sir," he replied.

"I'll come too," Shannon offered. "It will be faster to find Beth's trunk that way."

"We'll go straight home so that you and Shannon can rest from your journey," Mother promised Beth. "I'm sure you're longing for a hot bath."

"Thank you, Aunt Eleanor," Beth replied. "But

I must confess that we were pampered in New York last night. Shannon and I feel quite refreshed after our week of travel."

"I'm so glad to hear that," Mother said.

Hank and Shannon soon returned, followed by three porters wheeling the heavy trunk that Beth had brought with her.

While the porters strapped the trunk on top of the car, Hank held the door open for us. After Mother, Father, Beth, and I were settled, I noticed Shannon was hanging back, looking uncertain. Hank noticed too.

"Plenty of room in the front with me, if you don't mind, miss," he said to her.

A shy smile spread across Shannon's fair face. "I surely appreciate it," she replied.

"I was wondering if you heard any news about the assassination during your voyage," Hank started to say. Then he closed the door, and I couldn't hear any more of their conversation through the divider that separated the front of the car from our cozy cabin in the back.

As Hank pulled into the street, Beth craned her

neck to look past me out the window.

"Here," I said as I leaned forward. "You can see Providence better without me in the way."

"Oh, no, I wasn't looking at the city," she replied. "I was looking at *us*—our reflection in the glass."

I turned toward the window and realized that Beth was right; the window of the car was almost like a mirror. At first glance, a stranger on the street might not have guessed that Beth and I were related—after all, we were only third cousins. Beth had the most beautiful wavy hair, the color of an autumn bonfire. My hair was long, too—but dark brown and straight as sticks. Beth's creamy skin didn't have a single spot on it, whereas I had freckles enough for both of us.

But the longer I looked at our faces in the window, the more similarities I saw. We both had big eyes framed by long lashes and, best of all, identical smiles.

"You look so familiar," I blurted out. "I know it's not possible, but I almost feel like I've seen you before."

"I feel the same way," Beth confessed. "I suppose it's because I have imagined us doing things together for so long. And then, of course, I think about you every time I see your great-grandmother's portrait at

Chatswood. Do you have any portraits of my great-grandmother in your house?"

I shook my head. "No, and leaving them all behind at Chatswood is one of Great-Grandmother Katherine's regrets," I said.

"We don't really look like them. Our great-grandmothers both had blond hair—not ginger or brown," Beth said as she twirled a wavy lock around her finger. "But you did a splendid job describing yourself in your letters, Kate. You look exactly as I imagined you would."

Nellie's going to love Beth's accent, I thought. Then I noticed a flash of gold glittering against Beth's neck. I sucked in my breath. "Oh, Beth, that's it, isn't it? The Elizabeth necklace?"

Beth nodded, grinning as she pulled the Elizabeth necklace out of her dress. "I tuck it under my collar whenever we travel," she explained. "Just to be on the safe side. Want to see?"

"Of course I do!" I cried.

Beth unclasped the necklace and handed it to me. I was surprised by its weight; though the Elizabeth necklace looked like a delicate piece of jewelry, in my

hand it felt heavy. Solid. It was a perfect match to the Katherine necklace that Aunt Katie always wore: the other half of the same heart, the same burnished gold. The only difference was the gems, and oh, what a difference it was. Instead of the Katherine necklace's fiery rubies, ocean-blue sapphires shimmered against the Elizabeth necklace's gleaming gold.

"It's beautiful, Beth," I said, quickly passing it back to her. As much as I enjoyed admiring her Elizabeth necklace, it didn't seem right for it to be off her neck for even a second. "Absolutely beautiful. You must love it so much."

"I do. I truly do," she replied as she put the necklace back on. "You know, I've had it for less than a month, but I already feel like it's a part of me. I'm sure you'll feel the same way when the Katherine necklace becomes yours. Just two more days!"

"Don't I know it!" I laughed.

"Don't we all," Father teased as he glanced up from his newspaper. "I'm not sure what will occupy Kate's time once the countdown to her twelfth birthday is finally over."

"Me, I hope!" Beth said, giggling. "Do you know

when you'll receive the Katherine necklace? I was lucky; Mother gave it to me in the parlor, right after breakfast, so I didn't have to wait all day."

"That won't be the case for me, I'm afraid," I replied, glancing sideways at Mother. "They're not going to present it until my birthday party."

Mother smiled wryly. "Oh, Kate, it's not *my* rule. You know how much your great-grandmother lives for tradition. And ever since she gave the necklace to your great-aunt Kathy at *her* twelfth birthday party, the tradition was set. Besides, you've waited all these years; I'm sure a few extra hours won't cause any harm."

"If you say so," I said, sighing as though I were deeply inconvenienced. Beth gave me a sympathetic smile that told me she understood.

Then Hank pulled into the long, circular drive in front of Vandermeer Manor.

"Here we are," Father said.

Beth gasped. "Already?" she asked in surprise, leaning forward to peer out the window again. All the family and staff members were assembled in front of the house, awaiting her arrival. Hank parked the car and hurried around to open our door. I stepped out

first, and Beth followed me. At first, no one said anything; the only sound was the trickle of water streaming through the great fountain in the middle of the drive and, faintly, the call of the ocean.

And then, to my surprise, Great-Grandmother Katherine came forward, stepping out from behind Aunt Katie and Great-Aunt Kathy. Beside me, Beth gasped. As did I. I couldn't remember Great-Grandmother Katherine ever waiting outside to meet a visitor. Normally, she received our guests in the parlor.

Great-Grandmother Katherine moved toward Beth. "Elizabeth," she said slowly. "Beth. Great-granddaughter of my lost sister, standing on my steps, looking at me with her eyes."

Beth fell into a low curtsy, but my great-grandmother would have none of that. In a fast motion—faster than I'd ever seen her move before—she swooped down and gave Beth a great big hug. As Great-Grandmother Katherine held her, tears sparkled on Beth's long lashes.

"Happy tears, I hope," my great-grandmother said as she brushed them away. "Because this is a very

happy day for me, dear Beth."

"All my life, I've wished that I could've met her," Beth whispered.

"Of course, my dear girl. One of the many wrongs I've witnessed in this world is that Elizabeth left it before you arrived," Great-Grandmother Katherine said. "Look at you, child. Look at you. I feel as though you've unraveled all the long years of my life. Now I'm twelve again, too, with nothing to do but roam the meadows with my sister, looking for little adventures in the English countryside."

Great-Grandmother Katherine swept Beth's hair away from her face, leaned forward, and gently kissed her forehead. "I'm so glad you're here," she said.

"So am I," Beth murmured back.

And so am I, I thought.

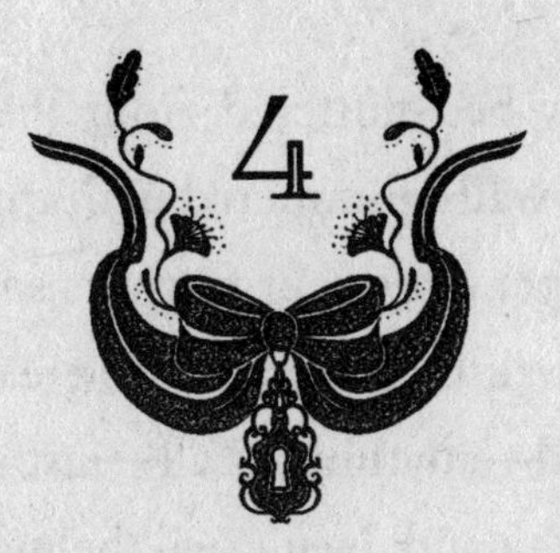

4

After Beth met the rest of the family, I led her inside Vandermeer Manor. "Mother's had the staff prepare the blue guest room for you," I told her. "But if you'd like, you're welcome to stay with me in my room."

"Yes, please!" Beth said at once. "I know two months seems like a long time, but it's only eight short weeks. I don't want to spend any time apart, if we can help it."

"I completely agree," I replied. "And I told Mother as much, too, but she said the proper thing to do would be to give you your own room—even though my room is certainly big enough for both of us. Here it is."

I swung open the door to my bedroom.

"Kate, it's beautiful!" Beth exclaimed.

I smiled. It *was* a very pretty room, especially on a bright summer day when the sunlight streamed through the open windows. The cream-colored canopy on my bed fluttered from the fresh breeze, and the green walls glimmered with thin gold stripes. The plush carpet under our feet was soft as velvet.

"I hope you'll be comfortable here. If there's anything you need—anything at all—just say the word. I know my lady's maid, Nellie, will be more than happy to help you. In fact, she'll never forgive me if I don't ring for her right away. . . . She's been just as eager to spend time with you as the rest of us!"

"No, no, you mustn't bother her on my account," Beth replied. "I'd hate to disturb Nellie when we have no real need of her."

"But it wouldn't be—" I started to say, but my voice trailed off. I didn't want to disagree with my cousin so soon after we'd met. *And maybe they do things differently in England*, I thought.

I decided to change the subject. "I got your letter—the one you sent before you set sail," I said. "You've got to tell me, what was the special item you said you'd bring?"

"Oh! Of course," she cried. "I nearly forgot. It's in my valise. Come. We must find it right away."

"The footmen probably brought it to your room," I told her. "It's right down the hall."

Beth followed me to the blue room, where we found Nellie and Shannon unpacking Beth's trunk. Even though they wore different uniforms, I was struck by how much Nellie and Shannon looked like each other as they unfolded and refolded Beth's clothes. And the way they spoke—in hushed voices, punctuated by giggles—immediately caught my attention.

"Nellie," I said. "Look who I've brought!"

"Lady Beth!" Nellie scrambled to her feet. "I'm at your service, milady. Should you need anything—anything at all—"

Beth smiled at her. "That's very kind; thank you. And thank you for taking Shannon under your wing as well." Then Beth turned to her lady's maid. "What were you two talking about?"

Nellie and Shannon exchanged a glance. The silence before Shannon answered seemed too long.

"Lady Beth, Nellie tells me that Vandermeer Manor is haunted," Shannon said at last.

"Really!" Beth exclaimed. "Do tell!"

Shannon shivered, despite the warmth of the day. "I daren't," she replied with wide eyes. "Haunts don't like to be the subject of gossip. And I'd rather not

make an enemy of Vandermeer Manor's otherworldly inhabitants."

Beth turned to me. "You're not so superstitious, are you, Kate?" she asked. "I should like to hear all about it."

"Well . . . ," I began. The memory of the specter I'd seen that morning was fresh in my mind. "It's just . . . stories, really. The housemaids . . . like to tell stories. To occupy themselves while they clean. But I've—"

My throat felt tight. I had to swallow hard before I could continue.

"I've never seen anything out of the ordinary," I finished lamely.

"Oh," Beth said. She sounded a little disappointed. "Yes, that's just how it is at Chatswood. The housemaids are always going on about this portrait tilting or that door closing, all performed by unseen hands. But the house seems ever so ordinary to me."

"And a good thing, too," Shannon added fervently.

I looked up and realized that Nellie was watching me closely. "Anything you need, Miss Kate?" she asked in a low voice.

I smiled at her; Nellie knew me so well. She must have seen how troubled I was by the talk of ghosts.

"I'm fine, Nellie; thank you," I replied.

"Shannon," Beth said. "Have you seen my valise?"

"Over here, milady."

Beth unfastened the leather strap holding it closed and removed a battered-looking book. Her eyes twinkled as she held it up for me to see.

"What is that?" I asked curiously.

Beth smiled in a secretive way. "Shannon," she said, "when you're finished here, would you please draw me a hot bath? I'd like to wash up before dinner."

"Of course, milady," Shannon replied. "Would you like to wash your hair as well?"

Beth shook her head. "Gracious, no," she said. "My waves are wild enough today. If I wash them, they'll spring out in every direction!"

"Nellie might be able to help with that," I spoke up.

My lady's maid blushed as everyone turned to her.

"My own hair is rather curly," Nellie explained. "So I've concocted a pomade that smooths curls."

"I'd love to try it," Beth said. "Thank you, Nellie." Then she turned to me. "Kate, I'd like to take a look at your stamp collection."

I understood what Beth meant. "Certainly. It's in

my room," I told her. "Let's go."

Beth and I ran down the hall, giggling. Back in my room, she placed the book on my bed.

"I really would like to see your stamp collection," Beth said. "But first, this is the surprise I wrote about in my letter."

I reached for the book. It was very old, held closed with a string of twine wrapped around its cracked leather covers. Tiny slips of paper peeking out of its pages served as bookmarks. "What is it?" I asked.

"It's a journal," Beth explained as she opened it and gently turned the pages, which were yellow with age. "Some sixty years old. It belonged to a woman named Essie Bridges . . . who was Elizabeth and Katherine's lady's maid when they were girls."

"Really?" I gasped.

"Yes, I'm sure of it," Beth replied. "She uses code names for them—most likely, Essie was scared that she'd be caught keeping a journal—but there's never been another set of twins at Chatswood. It's just got to be them! Here, read this."

The twins only look more alike with every passing day. I saw them at their ritual today, and with both of them wearing the same yellow dress with their hair in plaits, I could tell them apart only by their necklaces. It's the sweetest moment of my day, by far—first Sparrow holds up her necklace and says, with all solemnity, "I am Sparrow, and I love my sister, Lark." Next comes Lark's turn, and she holds up her necklace and says, "I am Lark, and I love my sister, Sparrow." Then together, they whisper, "Forever," and join their necklaces as one. It gives them a bit of comfort. They've been so brave, but I know they miss their mother very much.

"You're right," I said when I finished reading. "It has to be them."

"Now read this," Beth said, turning to an earlier page in the journal.

It was the twins' twelfth birthday today. After breakfast, Peacock presented Sparrow and Lark with Partridge's last gifts to her girls. The twins' faces were transformed by wonderment as they each opened a jewel box that contained a golden pendant. Lark's necklace is bejeweled with the most beautiful blue sapphires—her favorite color—while Sparrow's locket glitters with rubies. How well dear Partridge knew her girls! And how much she would've wanted to see their delight when they received this precious gift. That wasn't all, though. To each girl, Partridge had written a final letter. As much as Sparrow and Lark love their necklaces, they cherish those letters above all else.

"So sad," I whispered. It wasn't something Great-Grandmother Katherine talked about much, but I knew that the death of their mother had been very hard for her and her sister.

"I know," added Beth.

We sat quietly for a few moments. Then something

occurred to me. "I've never heard about those letters before," I said.

"Neither have I," replied Beth. "Don't you think that's odd?"

"Yes," I agreed. "It says right here that the letters were precious to them. The last words of their mother—"

"Almost as if she were speaking to them from beyond the grave," Beth interrupted me.

I tried not to shudder. I didn't want to think about that.

"Wouldn't the letters become heirlooms, too?" I asked.

"I would think so," Beth replied. "And, Kate, there's something else that's been puzzling me—the code names. I thought I had it all figured out—that Sparrow was Katherine and Lark was Elizabeth—but some things don't make sense. Like this passage, here."

Beth paused to turn back to the beginning of the journal, then read one of the entries aloud. "'My girls thought to play a clever trick on me by switching their dresses and hair bows. But since Sparrow tied her red ribbon around Katherine's wavy locks, I discovered their deception.'"

I sat up straight. "*Wait.* Did that say *Katherine's* wavy locks?"

Beth nodded.

"So Essie slipped and used one of the twins' real names," I continued. "But everyone knows that Katherine has straight hair. And red is her favorite color, not Elizabeth's. Which means . . . Katherine is Lark?"

"But Lark received the sapphire necklace," Beth said. "So Lark must've been Elizabeth."

"It doesn't make any sense," I said.

"Perhaps Essie was writing late at night and got the names—and the girls—confused. They were identical twins, after all."

"You know, there's one way to find out for certain," I said. "Why don't we ask Great-Grandmother Katherine? We could show her the journal—"

Beth held the journal to her chest protectively. "Oh, no, we mustn't do that!" she exclaimed.

"Why, Beth, it's been so many years," I said. "Surely there's no harm in her learning about it now."

"It's not that," Beth explained. "It's—ahem—how I found it. I was, ahh, how should I say this? I was

someplace I should not have been."

"Go on!"

Beth leaned forward and spoke in a whisper. "Chatswood Manor has a secret passage—perhaps more than one! Shannon showed it to me when I was investigating the disappearance of Cousin Gabby's necklace. That's where I found Essie's journal, hidden away in a crevice. But if Great-Great-Aunt Katherine sees it, she'll surely ask where I found it. And if word gets back to Mother and Father—"

"I understand completely. Don't worry. Your secret is safe with me," I promised my cousin. "I still think we should talk to Great-Grandmother Katherine. We won't mention the journal. But if she tells us what she and Elizabeth were like when they were young, maybe we can figure out which one of them really was Sparrow . . . and which one was Lark."

Beth nodded slowly. "Yes, Kate," she said. "Yes, I think that's a very good idea."

"Great-Grandmother Katherine always paints in the garden before tea," I told Beth. "We're sure to find her there. She loves talking about her sister . . . and I'm sure she'll be happy to answer our questions."

Shortly before it was time to start getting ready for dinner, I brought Beth to the garden nook where my great-grandmother liked to paint. Her easel and palette were set up in their usual spot, but Great-Grandmother Katherine was nowhere to be seen.

"Hmm," I said. "Let's go downstairs to see if Gladys, her lady's maid, knows where she is."

"Go downstairs?" Beth look scandalized. "Is that allowed?"

"Allowed? Of course it's allowed," I replied, giving her a funny look. "Why wouldn't it be?"

"Back home, I'm never allowed downstairs," Beth told me. "I've gotten ever so many lectures for sneaking down there. It's practically written in stone: The family stays upstairs where we belong."

"Really?" I asked. "But it's your house—even the downstairs."

"That's what I thought, but everyone says differently."

"Well, you're in America now," I said. "And here, there's nothing wrong with going downstairs."

I brought Beth down the servants' staircase. I peeked in the servants' common room, but I didn't see Gladys, so I decided to check the kitchen.

"Hello, Mrs. Hastings," I called out to our cook.

"Hello, Miss Kate," she called without looking up from the piecrust she was rolling on the counter. But when Mrs. Hastings saw Beth standing beside me, she let go of the rolling pin, and her mouth turned into a perfect, round *O*.

"Is this the Lady Beth?" she asked in astonishment as she wiped her floury hands on her apron. She dropped into a deep curtsy. "It's an honor to meet you, milady. An honor and a privilege. If there's anything you need—"

"Actually, Mrs. Hastings, we were wondering if you'd seen Gladys," I said.

She shook her head. "No, not since breakfast," she

replied. "But you might ask Mrs. Taylor."

"Thank you. I think we will," I said.

"Wait!" Mrs. Hastings called after us. She wrapped something in a napkin and hurried over to us. "These are for the picnic tomorrow, but you can have a few now. In case you feel peckish before dinner."

"Chocolate cookies?" I guessed.

Mrs. Hastings winked at me, and that was all the answer I needed.

"Well, Beth, are you hungry?" I asked as we walked into the hall.

"What's a cookie?" Beth said. "I do love chocolate."

"You don't know what a cookie is?" I asked in surprise. "They're delicious, is what they are—sweet, you see, and chewy . . . or sometimes crunchy. . . ." I held one up to show her.

A look of recognition crossed Beth's face. "Ohhh, so *that's* a cookie. In England, we'd call it a biscuit." She giggled.

"A biscuit? Really?" I asked. "That's something entirely different here."

When we finished eating our cookies, we crossed the hall to Mrs. Taylor's office.

"Mrs. Taylor is our housekeeper," I reminded Beth, just in case she had forgotten in the whirlwind of introductions. "She knows *everything* that happens at Vandermeer Manor."

"How funny that your housekeeper and your butler have the same surname," Beth mused.

"Funny? Not at all," I replied. "They are married, after all."

Beth stared at me in amazement. "Married? To each other?" she exclaimed.

"Of course! It's really very sweet—they met here five years ago and fell in love. They were wed right here in our English garden, and we had a little party for them afterward. It was so much fun, even though Mother made me dance with Alfie and he stepped on my toes."

"I don't think that's ever happened at Chatswood," Beth replied.

I put my finger to my lips as we approached Mrs. Taylor's door. I knocked swiftly to get her attention.

"Good afternoon, Lady Beth and Miss Kate," she said as she rose from her desk. "How may I help you?"

"Good afternoon, Mrs. Taylor," I replied. "We've

been looking for Great-Grandmother Katherine or Gladys. Do you know where they are?"

"Yes. Mrs. Vandermeer received an urgent message—something to do with preparations for the parade tomorrow. She left at once to attend to it, and Gladys accompanied her."

"Oh, I see," I replied. "When Gladys returns, would you let her know that we'd like to see Great-Grandmother Katherine?"

"Of course, Miss Kate," Mrs. Taylor said.

Just then, Anton poked his head into the room. "Pardon the interruption," he apologized, "but there is a delivery cart waiting outside, Mrs. Taylor. It has brought a large amount of lobsters."

"No, no, no," Mrs. Taylor said. "The lobsters are for Kate's birthday party, and they're not supposed to be delivered for three more days!"

Beth and I exchanged a glance, our eyes wide, as Mrs. Taylor hurried after Anton. "Excuse me for leaving so abruptly, but I've got to straighten this out at once," she called over her shoulder.

"Of course, Mrs. Taylor, not to worry," I called back. Then I turned to Beth. "We'll talk to

Great-Grandmother Katherine at dinner instead. I overheard her telling Mrs. Taylor that she wanted to sit next to you . . . and of course I'll be on your other side."

"Good," Beth said firmly as she linked her arm through mine. "That's exactly what I was hoping."

As it turned out, though, we didn't see my great-grandmother at dinner. Preparations for the parade kept her away from Chatswood until long after dessert had been served. And since she had been out so late, it was no wonder that she took breakfast in bed the next morning. The rest of us rushed through the meal so that we wouldn't miss a moment of the parade.

We made quite a parade ourselves as we left Vandermeer Manor—Mother and Father, Aunt Katie and Great-Aunt Kathy, Alfie, and Beth, and me. Then came nearly every servant, from Mr. and Mrs. Taylor to the kitchen maids. No one who lived or worked at Vandermeer Manor would dream of missing Bridgeport's Fourth of July parade!

Beth cast a worried glance over her shoulder. "What about Great-Great-Aunt Katherine? Isn't she

coming? Shouldn't we wait for her?"

"Don't worry about her," I told her. "Hank already drove her to the start of the parade route this morning. She has an important role to play."

"Really?" Beth asked curiously. "What do you mean?"

"Well, every year, the first float in the parade is called Great Moments in American History," I explained. "Great-Grandmother Katherine always dresses up as Martha Washington—you know, President George Washington's wife—and she sits on a velvet chair and waves to everyone in town."

Beth's mouth dropped open. "She *does*?"

"She loves it," I said. "In fact, I'm not sure who enjoys it more—Great-Grandmother Katherine or the people of Bridgeport. Everyone always claps and cheers when she comes by. I think it's because she's done so much good for the town. I've heard the house-maids say that no one in Bridgeport has ever gone cold or hungry since my great-grandmother came to stay at Vandermeer Manor."

"That's a bit like it is in England," Beth said thoughtfully. "Chatswood Manor is more than just

a house. There's a whole community of people who depend on it . . . and us."

We soon arrived at Main Street, where crowds of people had gathered on the sidewalks to watch the parade. Bright swags of bunting in red, white, and blue decorated every storefront, and cheery red bows had been tied around the streetlamps. The gazebo had been roped off with red and blue ribbon for us. Beside it, Hank was saving spots for the servants beneath a shady sycamore. And he wasn't alone.

"Shannon!" Beth said in surprise. "How did you get here before us?"

Shannon's cheeks flushed pink. "I drove into town with Hank," she explained. "And your great-grandmother, Miss Kate. In case—in case she needed anything."

But attending to Great-Grandmother Katherine's needs is Gladys's job, I thought. I was about to ask if Gladys was all right when Mrs. Randolph rushed over to us.

"Where is she?" Mrs. Randolph cried. "Where is she?"

"Who?" I blurted out, forgetting my manners.

Mother leaned past me and asked, "Who are you looking for, Mrs. Randolph?"

"Mrs. Katherine Vandermeer, of course!" Mrs. Randolph exclaimed. "The parade's about to begin, and we've lost our Martha Washington!"

Aunt Katie grasped Great-Aunt Kathy's arm. "Heat stroke?" she whispered anxiously. I bit my lip from worry. I knew how dangerous heat stroke could be, especially for a person of my great-grandmother's age.

"Hank," Father called. "You brought my grandmother to the start of the parade route, correct?"

"Yes, sir," Hank replied. "I left her there with Gladys."

The concern melted away from Father's face. "If she's with Gladys, she's fine," he declared.

"But what about the parade?" Mrs. Randolph wailed. "We need our Martha Washington!"

"If the parade cannot be delayed, perhaps you could take her place," Mother suggested. "I'm sure Katherine would understand."

"Well . . . ," Mrs. Randolph began. I could tell how much the idea appealed to her. Then her forehead

creased with frustration. "But there's no time to get into costume!"

Mother leaned up to whisper something in Father's ear, then stepped out of the gazebo. Her lady's maid, Ruthie, and Mrs. Taylor followed her. "Let's see if we can't all help you," she said to Mrs. Randolph as she led her toward the start of the parade route.

Beth and I exchanged a glance.

"I do hope Great-Great-Aunt Katherine's all right," Beth said. "Where could she be?"

"I have no idea," I said. Then I noticed Father speaking to Great-Aunt Kathy and Aunt Katie in a low voice. My aunts looked, suddenly, very relieved. *What is going on?* I wondered. But before I could ask, I heard a new sound: the bright, chipper notes of "Yankee Doodle."

"Beth!" I exclaimed. "The parade is starting!"

She craned her neck to look down the street. "I see it!"

First came Edgar Mason and Vincent Cleary, who carried the Town of Bridgeport banner. As the crowd cheered, the Great Moments in American History float followed. Every year, I laughed to see Dr. Wilson dressed up in a powdered wig as

President Washington, and Mr. Howard, the grocer, made a splendid President Lincoln. Normally Great-Grandmother Katherine was my favorite part of the float—but today, she was missing. Instead, Mrs. Randolph, the Martha Washington wig slightly askew on her head—waved to the crowd in her place.

But where was Great-Grandmother Katherine?

A brass band followed the float, their instruments flashing in the sun as they played patriotic music. Next came members of the Garden Club, tossing red, white, and blue flowers at the crowd. Then came . . .

I gasped and clutched Beth's arm. "Do you see that?" I shrieked. "It's—"

"It's her!" Beth finished for me.

There she was, Great-Grandmother Katherine herself, walking proudly and gracefully behind a new banner, one that I'd never seen at the parade before.

It read: SUFFRAGETTE SISTERHOOD OF BRIDGEPORT.

My mouth dropped open. "But—how—" I stammered. "Beth—"

"She really is as wonderful as you said," Beth said, watching with admiration.

"You don't understand," I said, still shocked.

"They—they—Mrs. Randolph forbade the suffragettes from marching. But look at them now!"

"I'd wager that my grandmother has a bit more sway over popular opinion than Mrs. Randolph," Father chimed in. "She always has, and she always will."

Just then, Great-Grandmother Katherine spotted us in the gazebo. "Come on, girls!" she called, waving us over as she walked past. "What are you waiting for? I'm doing this for you! For all of us!"

"Oh, Father, may I join her?" I cried.

"I suppose so," he replied with an indulgent smile. "Your mother already has."

That's when I noticed that Mother was marching with the suffragettes too!

Beth and I grabbed hands and ran into the street. We stood on either side of Great-Grandmother Katherine behind the large banner.

"Great-Grandmother Katherine," I began. "Didn't Mrs. Randolph deny the Suffragette Sisterhood's application?"

"Oh, that?" she said. "Yes, yes, she did. When word reached me, I knew that I'd missed the wrong meeting of the Bridgeport Beautification Society. The people of

this town may not agree on every issue, my dear, but we don't silence others' opinions. Your great-grandfather wouldn't have stood for that, and neither will I."

"But how did—?"

"I called on the Suffragette Sisterhood and told the members that they had my full support, and if there was anything I could do for the cause, I was at their service. So when the ladies needed a few extra hands yesterday to finish sewing the banner, Gladys and I came right away."

"*You* sewed it?" Beth asked in surprise.

"I certainly did," Great-Grandmother Katherine said proudly. "I helped, at least. Pricked my finger three times but didn't get a speck of blood on the banner. My lady's maid at Chatswood Manor taught me well."

Beth and I exchanged a glance behind Great-Grandmother Katherine's back.

I looked up at my great-grandmother. "Your lady's maid?" I asked, prodding her a bit.

"Oh, yes, Essie Bridges," my great-grandmother replied. "A kinder soul I have yet to meet."

From the other side of Great-Grandmother Katherine, I could see Beth nodding her head at the

confirmation that the writer of the journal she found in Chatswood Manor was indeed lady's maid to our great-grandmothers.

As we marched, the sun warmed my face; my steps kept time to the rousing sounds of the brass band as the claps and cheers of the crowd rang in my ears. Plenty of faces in the crowd frowned at us; I caught more than one man shaking his head in disgust. But it seemed to me that just as many people grinned to see us marching . . . or at least watched us with interest. A few eager supporters even threw the Garden Club's blooms back to us! I wasn't sorry to miss out on watching the rest of the parade—it was much more fun to be part of it. And no one enjoyed the parade more than Great-Grandmother Katherine, waving, calling out greetings to everyone she saw, encouraging others to join us behind the Suffragette Sisterhood banner. I felt a surge of pride as I marched along beside her. I already knew that I would never forget this moment for as long as I lived.

And best of all, the Fourth of July celebrations were just beginning!

After the parade, Mayor Watson took to the

platform in Town Square to read the Declaration of Independence in his deep, booming voice. The solemn words always gave me a thrill. But today I glanced sideways at Beth. I hoped she wouldn't be offended, especially by the parts that talked about the tyranny of King George. Luckily, Beth didn't seem upset. She was listening with her eyes closed, a look of respect on her face.

After that, there were a few rousing speeches, and then the brass band struck up again, playing "My Country, 'Tis of Thee." We all sang along, except Beth—though I noticed the hint of a smile playing across her lips. "I know that tune," she said to me when the singing finished. "But in England, it has very different lyrics. We call it 'God Save the King.'"

"But what if there's a queen on the throne?" I asked.

Beth grinned. "Then we call it 'God Save the Queen' instead!" she replied.

We walked back to Vandermeer Manor together, following my parents, with all the servants trailing behind us.

"I quite enjoyed your Independence Day," Beth said enthusiastically. "Can you believe we marched

in a parade? I wonder what Shannon will have to say about that. At home, everyone would have been scandalized—but it mustn't have been too bad if Great-Great-Aunt Katherine did it. It seemed as though the whole town adores her."

"Oh, they do," I said. "Everyone loves her. How could they not? She's always in the middle of everything—helping, organizing, arranging. Great-Grandmother Katherine makes good things happen. I can't imagine what Bridgeport would do without her.

"Wait till we get home,"I continued."Mrs. Hastings has fixed a picnic of American foods that you're going to love. And tonight, there will be a clambake and fireworks over the ocean!"

"What fun," Beth said, her eyes shining. "It seems the excitement never stops in America."

"Don't you—well, I suppose you don't celebrate the Fourth of July, of course," I said awkwardly.

"No, we don't," Beth replied. "But we have Guy Fawkes Night in November. He was part of the Gunpowder Plot to blow up Parliament and murder King James in 1605. But it was foiled, and we've

celebrated every year since. It's a grand time, with bonfires burning on every corner and fireworks lighting the night."

"Fireworks are my favorite," I said.

"Mine too," Beth said. "Do you think we might pop by the kitchen—in case Mrs. Hastings has any more of those biscuits? Or *cookies*, I should say."

I glanced around for Alfie, but didn't see him. "Yes, but we'd better hurry," I replied. "Because if Alfie knows about the cookies, there won't be any left."

Beth and I ran toward the house, laughing all the way. But our laughter faded as soon as we stepped inside Vandermeer Manor. Mother and Father were waiting for us, with grim expressions on their faces. I could tell right away that something was wrong.

"Come into the parlor, my dears," Mother said gently. "There's been a telegram from England."

Beth stayed rooted to the spot. All the color drained from her face, leaving her ashen and trembling. "What's wrong?" she asked. "What happened? Is it—is it Mother—or—?"

"No, no, no, nothing like that!" Mother said at once as she wrapped her arm around Beth. "Your family is

just fine—as well as can be."

A tremendous sigh of relief shook Beth's shoulders. "Then why did they send a telegram?"

"Please, Father, read it," I said.

He cleared his throat. "Europe unstable—stop—talk of war—stop—send Beth home at once—stop—confirm passage on earliest steamship to London—stop—Lord and Lady Etheridge," Father read from the paper in his hand.

Send Beth home at once.

In the silence that followed, those words reverberated, as if Father kept repeating them.

"Go home?" Beth said numbly.

"No!" I cried. "No. She just got here!"

"Kate," Mother began.

"Why does she have to leave?" I demanded. "The war hasn't started. There might not even be a war! And even if there were, Beth is safe here. Safer than she would be overseas!"

"Kate," Mother said again. "This is not our decision to make."

"You're right, of course," I said. "It's *Beth's* decision." I turned to my cousin. "What do you want to do, Beth?

Would you prefer to go home?"

She shook her head vehemently. "No, Kate, never!" Beth exclaimed.

"Please," I begged my parents. "Please don't send her away. We've waited so long for this—and she's only just arrived—it's not fair—"

Father and Mother exchanged a troubled glance.

"You know, Eleanor, the girls do have a point," Father said as he stroked his beard, like he always did when he was deep in thought. "I see no reason why Beth couldn't stay at Vandermeer Manor for the duration of the war . . . should such a thing come to pass."

"Lord and Lady Etheridge could not have been clearer," Mother argued. "I can imagine myself in Liz's shoes—if Kate were halfway across the world and war brewing—and I know that I would want my daughter by my side, safe beneath my roof, no matter what it took to bring her back."

"Here's what we'll do," Father announced. "We'll send a telegram to the Etheridges and assure them that Beth is safe here and welcome to stay until cooler heads prevail on the Continent. Most likely, they didn't want to impose on us. All right with you, Eleanor?"

In the moment before Mother answered, I held my breath. Beth did the same.

"Yes, of course," she replied at last. Then she fixed Beth with a welcoming smile. "We are honored to have you here and will see if we can keep you here for your fully planned stay."

"Thank you!" Beth and I cried at the same time as we swooped toward Mother, wrapping her in such a fierce hug that she nearly lost her balance. Father laughed as he used his strong arm to steady us all.

"If you'll excuse me, I have a telegram to compose," Father told us. "And then I think we all have a bit more celebrating to do. From what Mrs. Taylor tells me, Mrs. Hastings has outdone herself with a special Fourth of July picnic. I, for one, cannot wait to have some of her delicious cherry pie."

The next morning, there was a telegram waiting for Father at the breakfast table. Beth's parents had responded before dawn.

INSIST BETH RETURN HOME IMMEDIATELY STOP

CONDITIONS UNSAFE STOP PASSAGE BOOKED 6 JULY

EVENING

"My poor dears," Aunt Katie breathed.

"Again the wide ocean will separate two girls who should be together," Great-Aunt Kathy added sorrowfully. Great-Grandmother Katherine was unusually silent.

At last, I found my voice. "Six July?" I said in shock. "July *sixth*? But—that's tomorrow! My birthday!"

"I *won't*," Beth said stubbornly. "I *won't* leave on

Kate's birthday, and I *won't* miss her party."

"I'm afraid we don't have a choice," Mother said. "Lord and Lady Etheridge stand firm in their decision."

"But—" I argued.

"Anton, bring Hank," Father said over his shoulder. Then he turned to me. "Young lady, I understand that you're disappointed, but there is simply nothing else to be done. I can't say I blame Lord and Lady Etheridge. If a war broke out, I'd want my children safe at home."

"I'd go fight," Alfie spoke up.

"Shut it, you!" I snapped.

"Kate!" Mother reproached me.

Hank appeared in the doorway, wearing his uniform. "Yes, sir?" he said to Father.

"Change of plans, Hank," Father said. "Beth and—and—"

"Shannon," Beth spoke up.

"Yes, of course, Beth and Shannon will need to go to the train station at daybreak tomorrow," Father continued.

Hank flinched. "Beth and Shannon?" he repeated.

"Yes, they're returning to England tomorrow evening," Father said. "It will be a long and grueling day of

travel for them, I'm afraid, but at least Kate and Beth will be able to spend today together."

A heavy silence hung over us. At last, Beth spoke.

"Is there nothing else to be done?" she said. "Is there no way I might stay?"

"No," Father said, his voice gentle and firm at the same time. "I'm sorry."

Beth turned to me. "Then we'd better make the best of it, Kate," she said, her face stiff with determination. "I only wish . . ."

"What?" I asked.

Beth's smile was sad. "I only wish I'd been able to see you receive the Katherine necklace."

"And so you shall." Great-Grandmother Katherine finally spoke, with a steely glint in her eyes. "We might live by tradition in this family, but we don't die by it. You won't be twelve until tomorrow, Kate, but you'll receive the Katherine necklace at tea today."

Despite my sadness, I felt a sudden thrill. "Today?" I asked, hardly daring to believe I'd heard correctly.

Aunt Katie's fingers fluttered to the pendant hanging around her neck. "Yes," she said. "I've been looking forward to this since you were born, sweet Kate."

After we were excused from breakfast, I took Beth on a tour of Vandermeer Manor. The long, empty corridors were perfect for quiet chats that no one else could hear. On the second floor, we settled ourselves on a plush bench beneath the large picture window that overlooked the ocean. Beth stared at the rolling waves.

"I had hoped to go to the seashore," she said wistfully. "I wanted to look out at the waves to see if they were different on this side of the ocean."

As her voice trailed off, Beth frowned and leaned closer to the window. I thought at once about the ghost I'd seen. My pulse quickened. "Do you see—is someone out there?" I asked.

"Yes," she replied right away. "It's Shannon! Where is she going?"

We watched Shannon run from the house.

"Is she afraid?" I wondered. "She seemed upset when she first heard about the . . . haunting of Vandermeer Manor. Maybe she wants to get away for a spell."

Then Shannon turned her head to glance behind her. Who was she running from . . . or to?

"What *is* she doing?" Beth asked. Then she leaped

off the bench. "Come on," she cried. "Let's follow her!"

We ran through the hall toward the stairs, keeping an eye on Shannon through each window we passed until she disappeared through the hedge that led to the rose garden.

"Rats," I said, trying to catch my breath. "We won't find her now. By the time we get downstairs, who knows where Shannon will be?"

But Beth didn't answer me.

I turned around to see her kneeling next to a door in the wall. With a sinking feeling, I realized exactly where we were.

"Kate, do you see this?" Beth asked. "It's a door! This is just how the secret passage looks at Chatswood. Does Vandermeer Manor have a secret passage too?"

"No, it's not a secret passage," I said. "This door leads to the East Wing. It's closed; we have no need of these rooms. And no one ever goes inside." I reached for Beth's hand. "Come. Let's go down to the rose garden and see if Shannon's there."

Beth's eyes were shining with excitement. "Kate," she said urgently. "Why didn't we think of this sooner?"

"Think of what?"

"If no one ever goes in there, it's the perfect place for me to hide!" she exclaimed. "I won't have to leave Vandermeer Manor. I won't have to leave *you*!"

"No, Beth," I said, shaking my head. "It's a good idea—a great one, even—but there's something you don't know about the East Wing."

"What's that?"

I swallowed hard. "It's—it's haunted. There was a . . . a ship's captain lost at sea, long ago, and his ladylove waits for—"

Beth's laughter pealed through the hallway. "Oh, Kate, you goose," she said. "There's no such thing as ghosts."

"But everyone says—"

"I'm not a bit afraid," Beth said. "And even if your ghost captain and his ladylove did appear before me one day, I would point in the direction of the sea and send them on their merry way."

A small flame of hope flickered inside me. "I suppose . . . if you really want to stay . . ."

"I do," Beth said firmly. "I absolutely do."

"Then it just might work!" I exclaimed. "We would have to . . . tonight, while everyone's sleeping . . ."

"I'll hide away," Beth finished for me.

"There will be such a fuss in the morning when nobody can find you! Will you tell Shannon?"

For the first time, Beth looked troubled. "I don't know," she admitted. "I trust her, and I know she can keep a secret . . . but if your parents question Shannon, she might tell them everything. Then again, I wouldn't want her to worry about me."

"We don't have to decide that right now," I said. "In fact, we'll need to spend the rest of the day pretending that you're leaving tomorrow as planned. So act sad!"

"That won't be easy," Beth said with a huge grin.

"I'll need to bring you food," I said thoughtfully. "Mrs. Hastings keeps a close eye on her kitchen, but perhaps I can sneak extra food for you at each meal."

"I'm not picky," Beth assured me. "I don't care what I have to eat, as long as I stay right here until I'm supposed to leave next month."

Scritch. Scritch. Scratch.

Beth and I stared at each other with wide eyes.

The noise was coming from behind the door.

"Did you—" she whispered.

Scraaaaaaaaaaaaatch.

I grabbed Beth's hand. "Run!"

7

"It was just a mouse," Beth whispered as we raced to my room. "I've heard them in the walls at Chatswood. They make that noise when they scurry around. And I'm not afraid of mice, either."

"If you're sure," I whispered back. And then there was nothing more we could say about it, because Nellie was waiting for us.

"I was just about to send out a search party!" she exclaimed. "Come. We've got to get started, as I'll be attending to you both today."

When Beth looked at me with her eyebrows raised, I knew we were thinking the same thing. "Where's Shannon?" she asked, trying to sound casual.

Nellie turned away from us as she reached for a hairbrush. "Oh, she's packing for the journey," she said—but her voice sounded odd. "She thought you might want to wear your blue taffeta dress to tea, Lady Beth?"

"Yes, I think that would be lovely," Beth replied. "Shannon is so stylish. I'd wear anything she suggests."

But from the look on Beth's face, I could tell that she didn't believe that Shannon was packing.

Nellie buzzed around as busy as a bee, first helping Beth change into her gown, then helping me with mine. My tea dress was made of white cotton fabric with tiny red dots, trimmed with shiny red ribbons. I even had a matching satin hair bow. Beth and I sat close together on the bench in front of my vanity table while Nellie fixed our hair. Try as we might, we couldn't look sad; every time our eyes met in the mirror, one of us would smile, then the other, and then we would both start giggling so hard that we made it nearly impossible for poor Nellie to attend to her tasks.

"Please hold still, Miss Kate," she begged me. "Your hair is not easy to manage under the best of circumstances."

"I know." I sighed. "Straight and slippery—the worst of all worlds."

"But that's what makes it so beautiful," Beth said.

"I've never seen such shiny hair."

I smiled at my cousin in the mirror and noticed the light dance off her Elizabeth necklace. With a thrill I realized that I had to wait only a little longer for the Katherine necklace to sparkle around *my* neck.

"There," Nellie said at last. "You both look as pretty as a picture."

"Thank you, Nellie. Is it time, then?" I asked, feeling all fluttery inside.

"Yes," Beth said as she tucked a prettily wrapped present under her arm. "I'm so excited for you!"

We walked to the dining room, careful not to muss our dresses on the way. Everyone else was assembled—Mother and Father, Aunt Katie and Great-Aunt Kathy, Alfie with dirt smeared on the cuff of his shirt. *He's been busy catching frogs again*, I thought.

And Great-Grandmother Katherine was there, of course. She stood at the front of the room with her hands clasped.

"Kate," she said warmly. "The fourth Katherine Vandermeer. The moment you've waited for has finally arrived. Come here, dear girl."

I walked forward to join my great-grandmother. When I reached the front of the room, Aunt Katie rose with a velvet box in her hands.

"The time has come for the Katherine necklace to grace another," Aunt Katie announced. "As part of this tradition, with a heart full of love for my dear niece, I return the Katherine necklace to its original owner."

Great-Grandmother Katherine took the jewelry box from Aunt Katie and held up the Katherine necklace. Suddenly, I saw it with new eyes: the graceful swoops of the half-heart pendant dangling from a delicate chain; the rubies, sparkling with fiery light; the warm glow of the gold.

I closed my eyes as Great-Grandmother Katherine stepped behind me. One moment passed . . . two . . . three . . . and then I felt the Katherine necklace resting against my chest, a weight my heart would gladly bear.

I opened my eyes to see everyone looking at me: Father and Mother beaming proudly; Aunt Katie and Great-Aunt Kathy's eyes moist from their own memories of receiving the Katherine necklace; even Alfie's grin looked genuine for once.

Then there was Beth, wearing a wavering smile

as she tried to discreetly wipe away a tear. My cousin didn't need to tell me how much she missed her own great-grandmother at that moment. Her eyes said it for her.

Great-Grandmother Katherine must have noticed too. "Beth," she said suddenly. "Please join us."

Beth rose from the table and walked to the front of the room. Katherine faced us and held our hands.

"It has been a long time since the Elizabeth and Katherine necklaces were together," my great-grandmother said. "Too long. It is right that today we can admire them as they were meant to be: side by side."

There was a pause before she spoke again.

"Sometimes, though, there are forces that keep the necklaces—and those who wear them—apart," she continued. "Duty. Responsibility. Love. Sometimes those forces act in ways we don't understand. In ways that break our hearts. In ways that keep us far away from the people who are dearest to us."

Great-Grandmother Katherine stared straight at me. "There is no burden so heavy as a long-kept secret," she said. "It weighs more with each passing day. And there is nothing that can entirely heal

the ache of longing for one's homeland. If Beth stays at Vandermeer Manor, she might never return to England, to Chatswood, to home. She might never see her parents again."

Beside me, Beth stiffened slightly. I looked into my great-grandmother's eyes and thought: *How does she know about our plan?*

"You are standing on a threshold, Kate," Great-Grandmother Katherine said. "As you begin the journey into adulthood, let the Katherine necklace, and all the love and wisdom of those who wore it before you, guide your steps."

Great-Grandmother Katherine released our hands. "Enough pomp!" she declared. "I understand that Mrs. Hastings has outdone herself in the preparation of today's tea. Far be it from me to delay us any longer."

Beth and I slipped into our seats at the table as Anton and Emil wheeled in the tea carts. One was laden with eight individual pots of tea, along with tiny pitchers of cream and plates of sugar cubes that had been stacked into pyramids. The other cart was piled high with food—and, best of all, a tray of cupcakes, each one topped with a flickering candle.

Father began singing in his deep baritone voice. Everyone else joined in at once, and I blushed with pleasure to hear them all sing the "Happy Birthday" song to me. I closed my eyes as I tried to decide what I should wish for. The first wish I thought of—*I wish that we could all be together forever*—somehow seemed wrong, especially in light of what Great-Grandmother Katherine had said. So at the last moment, I changed my wish.

I wish we could always be as safe and sound as we are right now.

Then I took a deep breath and blew out the candles—every last one.

Beth stood up. "Kate, this is my birthday present to you," she said as she handed me the gift. When I opened it, I found a framed photograph of a portrait hanging on a wall.

"That's our great-grandmothers in the portrait," Beth explained. "It hangs in the parlor at Chatswood; I asked Father to take a photograph of it with his new camera. No one could remember if any of the portraits of the twins had made the journey to America with Great-Great-Aunt Katherine. So I wanted to bring

one with me—as best I could, anyway."

Everyone crowded around to see.

"I remember sitting for this portrait," Great-Grandmother Katherine said. "It was painted not long after our twelfth birthday. What a wonderful thing to see it again after all these years."

"Thank you, Beth," I said. "It's perfect."

While Anton and Emil served us, I glanced between the photo and the Katherine necklace. It was so strange to see the necklace sparkling against *my* dress; to realize that now I was wearing it, just as my great-grandmother had when *she* was twelve years old. I vowed then and there that I would wear it every single day until it was time to give it to the next Katherine in our family, whoever she may be. Perhaps Alfie's daughter, or perhaps even my own!

Throughout tea, I noticed that Beth was quiet. Afterward, we wandered through the halls to the East Wing.

"We should take a peek inside," I said. "Do you think it's locked?"

"Kate," Beth began.

I kept talking, as if my chatter could stop Beth

from saying what was in her heart. "Just to make sure it's a fitting place for you to stay."

"Kate."

"Of course, Vandermeer Manor has seventy-five rooms, so if those in the East Wing are not to your liking—"

"Kate."

Beth took my hands in hers.

"Kate, I can't stay," she said. Beth was hoarse, as if the words were sticking in her throat.

"I know," I whispered.

"If I *never* went home again . . . if I *never* saw Mother and Father . . ."

"I know."

"My whole life, I have missed my great-grandmother. I couldn't bear to inflict such pain on my own parents. They have called me home, and I must go to them. But I *will* come back," Beth promised. "And someday you'll come to me! Chatswood Manor is as much your history as it is mine, Cousin Kate. You should see it with your own eyes. You should sleep under the same roof where Elizabeth and Katherine grew up."

I nodded, not trusting myself to speak without crying.

"This war—if there is a war—it won't last forever," Beth said. "We *will* be together again."

"Yes," I finally said. "I know." I tried to smile, but I felt like my face would shatter. As much as I wanted to believe Beth, I was haunted by what had happened to our great-grandmothers. Once they had parted, they had remained apart for the rest of their lives.

What if the same thing happened to Beth and me?

An expression of urgency filled Beth's face. "Do you remember?" she asked. "From Essie's journal—the chant the twins used to say, when they put their necklaces together?"

"I think so."

"We'll do it now," Beth said. "Right here, to seal our promise that we *will* be together again."

I nodded my head and lifted the half heart of the Katherine necklace into the air. Beth faced me and did the same with the Elizabeth necklace.

"I am Beth, and I love my cousin Kate," Beth said solemnly.

"I am Kate, and I love my cousin Beth," I replied.

"Forever," we said at the same time.

A beam of sunlight shone through the window. It reflected off the rubies and sapphires, sending red and blue lights dancing across the wall.

Then a thin shiver crawled down my spine. I had the oddest feeling . . . that someone was listening nearby. . . .

Beside me, Beth rubbed her arms, which were covered with goose bumps.

"Do you feel it?" I whispered. "Like . . . like there's someone . . . here?"

"I do," Beth whispered back.

"Maybe it's the ghost."

"I wish it were Great-Grandmother Elizabeth." This time, Beth's whisper was so faint I wasn't sure I'd heard her correctly.

"We haven't finished the ritual," I replied.

Without speaking, we slid the half hearts together until they formed, at last, a single, whole heart.

Click. Click. Whirrrrrrrr.

The sound of a clockwork mechanism—the spinning of miniature gears—the creaking of a little-used hinge—

A tiny, unseen panel opened in the back of each heart.

A handful of confetti fluttered to the floor.

For a moment, neither of us moved.

Then I reached down, scooped up the snippets of paper, and together Beth and I walked hurriedly to my bedroom. My heart was thundering in my chest—and not just from how quickly we walked.

"What is it?" Beth asked.

My fist was trembling as I carefully unclenched my fingers. The yellowed papers drifted into a pile on my vanity table.

Beth lifted one up to the light. Squinting her eyes, she said, "There's something written on it . . . a letter *R*, I think."

"This one has an *E*," I announced as I examined another one.

"I have an *A*!"

"Another *A*! And a *T*!"

When we finished sorting the scraps of paper, Beth and I had found twelve in all: three *R*'s, two *A*'s, two *E*'s, and one each *F*, *P*, *O*, *V*, and *T*.

"It's a message," I said. "All this time, there's been a message hidden in the necklaces, and no one knew!"

"But what does it say?"

"I'm not sure," I admitted. "We'll have to unscramble the letters to figure it out."

We spent several silent minutes moving the letters into different arrangements but were no closer to deciphering the message than when we started.

"What if it's a code?" Beth suddenly suggested. "What if these aren't individual letters that form a message—but each one is an initial for a word?"

"But there must be thousands of possible words," I replied. "How would we ever figure that out?"

"We probably wouldn't," Beth said.

"It could even be a clue," I said. I swapped the *T* for the *P* and was about to move the *R* when there came a knock at the door. Quick as a wink, Beth covered the slips of paper with Essie's journal.

It was Nellie. "Sorry to bother you, ladies, but I was wondering if . . ." Her voice trailed off as she noticed

the Katherine necklace. "Oh, Kate," she breathed.

"Would you like to see it?" I asked.

Nellie traced her finger along the smooth edges of the half heart. "The most stunning jewels I've ever seen," she declared. "Those rubies! They sparkle like the sunset on the ocean. Kate, it suits you well. I'd say you were born to wear it."

"Thank you," I replied, beaming.

"Now, I didn't mean to interrupt you, but I was wondering if there's anything you need," Nellie said.

A frown flickered across Beth's face as she glanced at the clock. "Nellie, where is Shannon?" she asked bluntly. "I'm going to need help packing, and I think I'd like to take a bath before my journey."

"I can certainly help you, Lady Beth," Nellie replied, dodging Beth's question. "It would be my pleasure. And if you'd like, we could try the cider-vinegar rinse I use on my hair."

"If it's half so nice as the pomade you made, I know I'll love it," Beth said. She squeezed my arm as she rose from the vanity table. "I'll be back soon."

"I'll keep working on the puzzle," I said.

Alone in my room, I slid the letters across the table.

The *V* caught my eye. *V-E-R* . . . but there was no *Y*, so the word wasn't "very."

Then I spotted the other *E*. *E-V-E-R* spelled *ever*.

It was a start.

I kept swirling the letters—the *P*, the *A*, the other *R*'s—until I'd finally formed two words. But my thrill of triumph turned into a stab of disappointment when I realized what I'd spelled:

APART FOREVER.

No, I thought.

But there it was, staring at me plain as day. And though I hated to admit it, there was a terrible truth in those cruel words, because Katherine and Elizabeth had indeed been apart forever after my great-grandmother set sail for America.

Just like you and Beth will be apart forever after she leaves. The horrible thought ricocheted through my mind before I could stop it.

"No," I said aloud. With a sweep of my hand, the words disappeared, leaving a trail of scattered letters.

"Miss Kate?"

I jumped in my seat. The voice that called my name sounded faraway, almost ghostly. But when I spun

around, I found Shannon standing in the doorway. Her eyes were rimmed with red, and she wore an anxious expression. "Sorry to disturb you, but do you know where I might find Lady Beth?"

"I believe Nellie has drawn her a bath, and then they'll pack her trunks," I told her.

Shannon sighed in relief. "Very good. Thank you."

"You must be glad about the change of plans," I said.

"Beg your pardon?" Shannon asked, confused.

"Leaving early," I explained. "I know you're worried about the ghost. I imagine it will be a tremendous relief to depart in the morning."

Shannon's whole face seemed to crumple. Then, to my surprise, she began to cry!

"Shannon!" I exclaimed as I jumped up from the bench. I rushed to close the door, then led Shannon over to the comfortable armchair by the wardrobe. "What's wrong?"

Shannon took a deep breath to steady herself, but her chin was still trembling. "I'm—I'm—I'm in love!"

"In . . . love?" I asked in disbelief.

Shannon nodded miserably. "With Hank, the

chauffeur, Miss Kate. We—we spent the day together, yesterday and today, and . . . and . . ."

"Hank?" I repeated. I suddenly remembered the way Shannon had blushed when she stood close to him and the way Hank had flinched when he heard that she and Beth were leaving early. *Of course*, I thought. But what I said was, "Go on."

Shannon smiled through her tears. "He's the one for me," she said simply. "I never dreamed that I'd feel this way about anyone. And now . . . now I have to leave . . . and we've only just met. . . ."

Shannon covered her face with a handkerchief as she wept.

"There, there," I said as I placed my hand on her shoulder. "Shannon, if you love him, you should stay."

There was a long pause while Shannon tried to compose herself. "If it were that easy, I would," she replied. "But Lady Beth must return to England, and I'd never send her on such a journey all by her lonesome. I'd never abandon her like that."

An idea was beginning to unfurl in my mind. "And if . . . ," I began, "someone else could accompany Beth home. Someone we know and trust, would you stay?"

Shannon looked at me with shining eyes. "Yes, I would," she said. "Hank has my heart, always."

"You sit," I said as I crossed my room for my bottle of rosewater tonic. I splashed some of the fragrant liquid on a washcloth, then pressed it to Shannon's blotchy, tear-streaked face.

"No, Miss Kate," she said as she tried to pull away. "It's not right. I should be tending to you."

"Now, now, none of that," I said. "I have an idea, Shannon—an idea that might solve everything for you—but we'll have to act fast. So when you're ready . . ."

I offered Shannon a clean handkerchief. As she listened to my plan, she dried her eyes. Once I was finished speaking, Shannon took a deep breath and nodded.

"Then come with me," I said.

We found Beth and Nellie in the blue guest room. Beth was just out of the bath, wrapped in a velvet dressing gown while Nellie carefully combed all the tangles out of her long hair. "I don't know how you do it, Nellie," Beth was saying as she stared in the mirror. "My hair's *never* been so smooth and shiny before!

There's no frizzy bits at all! The waves in my hair look as calm as the ocean on a clear, warm day."

"All those years of battling with my own curls have finally paid off," Nellie replied with a laugh.

"I'm sorry to interrupt," I began. As quickly as I could, I explained Shannon's predicament.

Beth rose at once. "You can't leave, Shannon. You can't," she said firmly. "I won't have your heart broken on my account."

Shannon shook her head stubbornly. "I can't send you off all by yourself," she said, just as determined as my cousin.

"And that leads me to my plan," I spoke up. "Nellie, I don't quite know how to say this, but . . . would you consider going to England in Shannon's place?"

Everyone looked at me.

"What if you and Shannon were to switch places?" I pressed on. "She could stay here and be my lady's maid and . . . and maybe there would be another garden wedding at Vandermeer Manor before too long. And Nellie, you could accompany Beth to England and take Shannon's position at Chatswood Manor. Just think, you'd see your birthplace again after all these years and

meet your grandparents and your cousins at long last."

I looked at Nellie, who had yet to say a word. "But only if you truly, truly want to," I finished. "I couldn't bear it if you made the trip with a reluctant heart."

"Oh, Miss Kate," Nellie finally said. "I have no family here. I have no sweetheart. I have nothing but my fondness for you and your family. This is—this is—"

I held my breath as I waited for Nellie to finish.

"This is an opportunity I never dreamed to have," she said. "Yes, yes, of course I'll go, gladly. Though I have to be honest, Miss Kate. I'll miss you more than I can say."

I leaned forward and gave Nellie a hug. "And I, you," I replied, feeling the first prickle of tears in my eyes. "But you'll write to me, won't you, Nellie? And—and you'll see me again. Because I'll come to Chatswood Manor as soon as Mother and Father let me. I swear it."

"And you'll bring Shannon, I hope," Beth spoke up, her eyes welling up and her voice cracking. She walked over to her lady's maid and embraced her. "These are mostly happy tears, but I'm going to miss you terribly," she said.

"Of course I'll bring Shannon!" I said. "Now, we've got to hurry. There's so much to do—Shannon, I think it's best tomorrow if you stay out of sight until we know the ship has sailed. That way, no one will be able to interfere—"

"But surely Mr. and Mrs. Taylor will find out," Shannon said, a hint of worry in her voice. "What then?"

I shrugged. "I bet we can keep this under wraps for a while. You and Nellie look enough alike that it would be some time before anyone even noticed a switch, what with you wearing Nellie's maid's uniform. All you'd have to do is tone down your Irish accent a bit. By the time Mr. Taylor figured things out, everyone would know that no harm was done by making the switch. Now, Nellie—you'd best start packing—"

"I'll run and tell Hank," Shannon said. "He'll be as grateful as I am, Miss Kate. And then I'll return at once to help you finish packing, Lady Beth."

After Nellie and Shannon had left, I reached for the brush to help Beth with her hair. "Kate, you're American through and through," she declared. "I don't know how you came up with such a brilliant idea!"

It was still dark the next morning when I was awakened by a sliver of light shining through the doorway to my bedroom.

"Lady Beth. Miss Kate," Shannon whispered. "It's time to get up."

I bolted upright in bed. My twelfth birthday had arrived; that night, the entire town would arrive to celebrate. But what should've been the happiest day of my life had brought a tremendous sadness instead.

"Happy birthday, Cousin Kate," Beth said sleepily as she rubbed her eyes. "I wish I didn't have to go."

"So do I," I replied. I wiggled into the dress that Shannon had laid out for me.

"I'll have to say good-bye here, Lady Beth," Shannon said. "I can't risk being seen outside."

I didn't want to intrude on Beth and Shannon's last

moments together, so I excused myself and went downstairs. The stars were twinkling high above Vandermeer Manor when I found Hank and Nellie standing by the car. Nellie had left her uniform behind. Instead, she wore a simple blue dress with a gray traveling coat over it. The trunks had already been loaded; as soon as Beth came out, they would leave for the train station.

"I can't ever thank you enough, Nellie," Hank was saying, his cap in his hands. "This is a kindness that we'll never forget. We'll do our best to repay you."

"Nonsense," Nellie said. "I'm thrilled for this chance, Hank. A week from now I'll be in England!"

Then Nellie saw me. "Miss Kate," she began. She stopped, at a loss for words.

My smile felt crooked. "I suppose this is good-bye," I said. "Nellie, you've been—"

My voice trailed off. How could I begin to tell Nellie how much she meant to me? She'd been by my side for years now, helping me solve every problem, meeting my every need. I could hardly bear to face the reality that we would never again share a story in the stolen minutes of our days.

"You've been more than my lady's maid," I finally

said. "You've been my friend."

"And you've been mine," Nellie replied. "Please, Miss Kate, I know I've no right to ask, but you will keep in touch, I hope. I'd be so excited to receive a letter from you."

"Of course I'll write to you," I told her. "Otherwise, how will you ever find out the secrets of *The Hidden History of Castle Claremont*?"

Nellie grinned at me as I reached out to hug her. We both heard something jangle in her pocket.

"My keys!" Nellie gasped. "I almost forgot. Would you give these to Shannon? There's a key here for every lock in the house."

"Certainly," I replied as I took the heavy key ring from Nellie.

Then my cousin appeared in the doorway. My stomach clenched; the time to say good-bye had come.

Beth crossed the courtyard quickly. "Cousin Kate," she said. "It's not good-bye. It's *not.* I'll see you again soon; I'm sure of it."

"Yes," I said, wishing I could sound as certain as Beth seemed to feel. "I know."

"Listen. I left Essie's journal under your pillow."

"But—"

"I want you to have it," she said. "Maybe you'll find something that I missed. And keep working on the puzzle. I'm sure you'll be able to crack the code."

In those last moments with my dear cousin, I couldn't bear to tell her the truth: that the paper letters read APART FOREVER. Instead, I nodded, which was just as well, since the lump in my throat was making it hard to speak.

"Convince your parents to send you to England," Beth continued. "Better yet, all of you should come—even Alfie."

"I can't believe you're leaving," I said. "Your second transatlantic voyage in as many weeks. You're so brave."

My cousin shook her head. "I've always thought you were the brave one," she replied.

Hank cleared his throat. "I'm afraid it's time to go," he said quietly.

Beth threw her arms around my neck. "Write me!" she cried. "Write me every day! I love you, Cousin Kate. The last few days have been the most wonderful days of my whole life."

"Mine too," I said as I kissed my cousin on each

cheek. "Travel safely, dear Beth. Please—please send us a telegram when you arrive. And if war should come—"

Beth shook her head. "It won't," she said. "And even if it does, I'll be safe at Chatswood."

"Be careful all the same," I told her. "Nellie, take care of her for me, will you?"

"You have my word, Miss Kate," Nellie replied.

"Good-bye! Good-bye!" I called, waving so hard I thought my wrist would break.

Hank helped Beth and Nellie into the car, then closed the door behind them. I watched the car travel down the long driveway and turn onto the main road.

And just like that, they were gone.

The silence surrounding me was so steeped in sadness that I wasn't sure what to do. I knew Shannon was awake, hiding somewhere in the house . . . but I wanted to be alone. I wandered through the empty hallways until I found myself in the little alcove where Beth and I had joined our necklaces. Moonlight spilled through the window, casting a silver light over everything I could see. A few tears trickled down my face, but I wiped them away as fast as I could. I was twelve years old now, like my cousin, and I felt certain that *she*

wasn't crying in the back of the car. If Beth could be so brave to cross the Atlantic Ocean twice in two weeks, I could certainly buck up. I cupped my hands around the Katherine necklace. The cool weight of it made me feel better . . . a little better, at least.

Then something out the window caught my eye. I hardly breathed as I leaned forward for a closer look.

She was back.

And she was walking toward the house.

The mysterious figure moved slowly in the moonlight, once again dressed from head to toe in black. Her floor-length veil trailed behind her through the dewy grass. *It* is *Blythe Fontaine*, I thought. *She's spent the night searching the shore for her lost love.*

I was frozen to my spot; I felt as though I could do nothing but watch in horror as the ghostly figure approached Vandermeer Manor. Then, to my surprise, a second figure appeared. I squinted my eyes, trying to get a better look. It couldn't be—it wasn't possible—but—yes—

It was Great-Grandmother Katherine.

There was no mistaking her snow-white hair or the diamond-tipped sticks holding her hair in place. *But*

what is Great-Grandmother Katherine doing outside at this hour? I wondered, suddenly feeling more curious than afraid. The veiled figure seemed to fall into step alongside my great-grandmother. I remembered that unsettling feeling Beth and I had experienced the day before—the sense we had that someone was watching us. I'd thought it was the ghost of Blythe Fontaine, but she had wished it was her great-grandmother. Then the most astonishing thought struck me.

What if the ghost isn't Blythe Fontaine? What if it's . . . Elizabeth Chatswood?

I didn't dare blink.

Does Great-Grandmother Katherine see her? I thought as the pair moved, side by side, toward the East Garden. *Does she even know she's there?*

Before I could figure out the answer, they vanished behind the hedge.

My heart was pounding; my mind was whirling with questions. But I didn't feel frozen anymore.

I'm not sure what compelled me to move toward the door in the wall—the one that led to the closed-off East Wing. Then I realized that I needed to know just what was behind that door. I took a deep breath and

reached for the brass knob. It was locked, but that was to be expected. And it wasn't a problem.

After all, I had Nellie's keys.

The smallest, most tarnished key on the ring fit perfectly. I heard a series of small *clicks* as the key turned in the lock. Then the door swung open.

I stepped cautiously into the gloomy hallway. Heavy brocade curtains covered each window. They looked for all the world as though they hadn't been opened in decades. At the first door off the hall, I paused to listen. When I didn't hear anything, I turned the knob.

I'm not sure what I expected to find—perhaps an empty room where my footsteps would echo across a bare floor. Or perhaps clouds of dust would rise as I walked among the hulking shadows cast by sheet-covered furniture. But I know I never imagined that I'd step into a tidy and perfectly furnished sitting room, where the open windows admitted silver rays of moonlight. Three doors at the opposite end of the room made me believe I was in some sort of apartment.

These rooms aren't closed, I thought as I looked at the ticking clock on the writing desk, the tall bookshelf, and the comfortable settee crowded with embroidered

pillows. *They're very much in use. I think . . . I think someone lives here! But who?*

I stepped closer to the writing desk and reached for a shimmering silver chain. A dozen tiny attachments hung from it; they chimed as I lifted it off the desk. The necklace was as lovely as it was useful. The attachments included a tiny notebook and silver pencil, a thimble, a vial made of red glass, an oval locket studded with rubies, and even a tiny paint set.

I was about to try it on when something else caught my eye: a framed daguerreotype of two girls. With one glance I could tell that they were twins—and I knew exactly who they were.

"Hello, Katherine. Hello, Elizabeth," I whispered. They looked to be about my age, wearing lacy white collars on their dresses. Though the image was somewhat grainy, there seemed to be the hint of a chain around each girl's neck. Unfortunately, the daguerreotype had been cropped at their shoulders, so I couldn't know for sure if the twins were wearing their special necklaces. And with their hair woven into braids, it was impossible to tell which twin was which.

I studied the daguerreotype for several long

minutes; then, with a sigh, I put it back on the desk. The image had survived for decades and traveled thousands of miles, but there was nothing it could tell me.

Or was there?

I looked closer and saw a thin edge of paper peeking out of the frame.

Be still, I scolded my trembling fingers as I fumbled with the clasp on the back of the frame. It was stuck, as though it had been shut for many years; at last it gave, and I swung open the frame to reveal a folded piece of paper.

It was a letter.

I was about to read it when I heard something.

"I hope she won't be too grieved—"

"No doubt the disappointment cuts deep—"

A pair of voices at the other end of the apartment. And they were coming closer!

I shoved the daguerreotype back into the frame and jammed the clasp closed. Then I dashed away from the East Wing as quickly as I could, pausing only to wrench Nellie's keys out of the lock.

It wasn't until I had returned to my bedroom that I realized I was still holding the letter.

I paced back and forth. Who had I heard talking in the East Wing? Who were they talking about? Was my mind playing tricks on me . . . or did one of them sound like Great-Grandmother Katherine?

The letter. The letter. I turned it over and over in my hands. I knew that I shouldn't have it. I had no right to take it, let alone read it . . . but how could I resist?

9 January 1848

My dearest daughter,

The fates have not been kind to us, that my life should dim at the dawn of your adulthood. It is my greatest regret that I will not live to see you and your sister as women grown, married, perhaps mothers to girls of your own. I hold hope that the hole I leave in your life will be filled many times over with others who will cherish you as much as I do. Yet there may come times when you wish you could seek my counsel, and so I write this letter now for whenever you find yourself longing for your mother's advice.

This is it, I thought. *This is one of the letters that Great-Great-Grandmother Mary wrote to the twins and Essie Bridges mentioned in her journal.*

My sweet child, it has been my privilege to watch you grow for the past eleven—nearly twelve—years. And though your childhood has yet to end, your father and I have been charged with the challenging task of deciding your future. Let me assure you that our decision was made with great

care. When you are of age, you will marry your cousin, Maxwell Tynne, to fulfill the rules of inheritance. Maxwell is an honest and honorable young man and, I think, well suited for you. It is my great hope that your marriage will be a long and happy one, filled with love.

So this is Elizabeth's letter, I thought. *Elizabeth Chatswood, who married Maxwell Tynne and stayed in England as the lady of Chatswood Manor while my great-grandmother journeyed to America.* How strange that it had found its way to Vandermeer Manor when Elizabeth herself had never been able to make the trip. *Maybe Great-Grandmother Katherine inherited it after Elizabeth passed away*, I thought. But in that case, why was it in the East Wing—and not my great-grandmother's room?

I wonder if you have noticed yet how others look to you to lead them. Doubtless

they are drawn to your strength, which I see reflected even in the fiery hues of your favorite color. Your dedication to your family; your commitment to everyone you meet; your compassion for those less fortunate. Daughter, you have been graced with all the characteristics you will need as the next lady of Chatswood Manor.

I paused. Fiery hues . . . that must mean red. But everyone knew that red was Katherine's favorite color. After all, I was wearing the ruby Katherine necklace at this very moment. So this letter must have been written to . . . Great-Grandmother Katherine? Now I was thoroughly confused.

The hour grows late, and I still have one more letter to write before I retire. And so, my darling Elizabeth, I will conclude here. Please know today, tomorrow, and every day of your life how very proud you've made me

and how very much I love you.

Your loving mother

A sudden chill overtook me as the words blurred before my eyes. *So this really* is *Elizabeth's letter,* I thought in astonishment. *How in the world did it end up in a hidden-away room of Vandermeer Manor?*

My teeth were chattering; my toes felt like ice. The sun was just starting to rise, but I felt like I'd been up for an entire day. Even though I'd already gotten dressed, I crawled back into bed and pulled the comforter all the way up to my chin. I was so lonesome, missing my cousin and Nellie, who were already on the train to New York. A few tears spilled from my eyes, soaking into the satin pillowcase. *Don't*, I told myself fiercely. *Don't start.*

At some point I must've fallen asleep, because the next thing I heard was footsteps in my room and a voice saying my name.

"Miss Kate!"

"Nellie, I'm awake," I mumbled. "I'm awake."

"It's not Nellie who's calling you. It's me, Gladys."

I bolted upright in bed. Of course—Nellie was

gone now, and so was Beth. And if Gladys, my great-grandmother's lady's maid, had come to fetch me—

"What time is it?" I asked, squinting at the clock. "Two o'clock? In the *afternoon*? Why didn't anyone wake me?"

Gladys raised an eyebrow. *Of course,* I thought. *Who* would *wake me, with Nellie gone and Shannon hiding?*

"You're wanted downstairs," Gladys said. Her tone sounded ominous.

"Why—for what—" I stammered.

"Everyone knows. About Nellie."

"Oh," was all I said. I followed Gladys down to the parlor, where I found Great-Grandmother Katherine, Father, Mother, Mr. Taylor, and Mrs. Taylor waiting for me. Shannon stood against the wall, with her head bowed. She refused to meet my eye.

"Kate," Mother said, breaking the tense silence in the room. Her tone was clipped. I could tell she was angry. "How could you think Mrs. Taylor wouldn't notice that one of her maids went missing? Where is Nellie?"

I took a deep breath to steady my nerves. I hated to see my mother upset. "In New York, I guess."

"So you knew about this cockamamy plan?" Father

asked. His face looked stern, but I could see his eyes twinkling.

"It's not funny, William," Mother said. "I don't even know where to begin. How will we tell the Etheridges that we've sent a stranger to serve their daughter and live in their home?"

"Nellie's not a stranger," I spoke up.

"She's a stranger to *them*," Mother replied.

"So what if one lady's maid swaps with another—I don't see the problem here," Father said.

"If I may, sir, it reflects poorly on the house," Mr. Taylor said. He pulled off his spectacles and wiped them nervously with a large handkerchief.

I felt a sudden pang of remorse as I watched Mr. Taylor fiddle with his specs. We all knew about the trouble he had with his sight, despite the pains he took to hide it. It had never occurred to me that our little switch would make him feel foolish.

"They'll think that Mrs. Taylor and I don't have control of the staff, that such shenanigans are acceptable at Vandermeer Manor. And all because of a lovesick chauffeur and an impulsive lady's maid!" he continued.

"Mr. Taylor," Mrs. Taylor said reproachfully. "Perhaps you and I should not be so quick to judge."

"I completely agree," Great-Grandmother Katherine announced. "And on Kate's twelfth birthday, no less! What a tempest in a teapot."

Everyone turned to look at her.

"I assume Nellie has free will," my great-grandmother continued. "Perhaps she should've given proper notice, but if she chooses to vacate her position, so be it. I should think that if Nellie was good enough to serve our Kate, she's good enough to serve anyone, anywhere—even at Chatswood Manor. And I ought to know. Really, it's a tremendous stroke of good fortune that we had such a capable young lady willing and able to assume the role on such short notice. That's you I'm talking about, Shannon. No need to stand there looking shamefaced. You're not the first lass to fall in love, and you'll not be the last."

"And what should we say to the Etheridges?" asked Mother. "We'll need to prepare them for this surprise."

"Someone must send a telegram. Then I shall write a longer letter to them myself," Great-Grandmother Katherine declared. "I intend to provide Nellie with a

glowing letter of reference. Unless anyone disagrees?"

No one spoke.

"Good. Then, it's settled," my great-grandmother declared as she slowly rose from her chair. "Now, if memory serves, we are hosting the social event of the season tonight, and not a one of us is ready yet. Mrs. Taylor, perhaps you might arrange for a tray of savories to be sent to Kate's room, seeing as she's missed breakfast *and* lunch. And Shannon, lift your head, child. This is your chance to show everyone what an asset you'll be to our family. Gladys, I'd like to go to my room now."

Gladys helped my great-grandmother to the door. Then she paused. "And would someone please do something about my great-grandson?" she called over her shoulder. "If I'm not mistaken, he's spent the morning transplanting frogs into the fountain."

I gasped. "Mother, no! We can't have *frogs* leaping out of the fountain during my party!"

"And we won't," Mother said grimly. "We'll take care of it, Kate. Run along now—it's past time for you to start getting ready."

Shannon curtsied to everyone in the room before

following me into the hallway.

"I'm so sorry, Miss Kate!" she whispered. "I didn't mean for everyone to realize so quickly that Nellie and I switched. Mrs. Taylor—"

"Knows what everyone's doing at all times," I finished for her. "Don't worry, Shannon. I wasn't thinking clearly last night. I suppose it was awfully foolish for us to think we could hide the truth for more than a few hours."

"Everyone's been in such a tizzy today," she replied. "More deliveries than you can shake a stick at, the footmen running to and fro. . . . The housemaids said that even the *ghost* is restless today."

I stopped short. "*What*?"

"Oh, you know, bumping into things and making a racket up in the East Wing," Shannon said airily. "Lucy Jane said it's searching for something, the poor lost soul."

The ghost knows, I thought. *The ghost knows I was up there. Does she know I have the letter?*

"You know, it's funny. Hank told me that . . ." Shannon's voice trailed off as she looked at my face. "Oh, no, Miss Kate, now I've gone and upset you on

your birthday!" she cried. "It's just stories they tell to pass the time. I'm sure of it. The housemaids at Chatswood do the same. Don't be frightened."

"I'm not frightened," I replied. "Just . . . curious. If it's not a ghost, then what is it?"

"Not something for you to worry about on your special day," Shannon said firmly. "Now, here's what we'll do. I'll pin up your hair and draw you a nice, piping-hot bath. It'll melt all your cares away. Next you'll have your tray of nibbles, because your great-grandmother's quite right. It would never do for you to faint at your very own birthday party."

"I *am* really hungry," I admitted.

"And then we'll get you ready for your big night," Shannon said. "I'm an old hand at such things, you know."

"That's right," I said. "You helped Beth get ready for her twelfth birthday party, didn't you?"

Shannon nodded. "And it will be an honor to do the same for you. Come along, Miss Kate."

For the next five hours, Shannon clucked over me like a mother hen. So much had happened since the early morning—saying good-bye to Beth and

Nellie, spotting the ghost, sneaking into the East Wing, taking the letter—that it felt good to let someone else do the worrying for a bit. I ate one of the sandwiches Mrs. Hastings had made for me while Shannon worked on my hair.

I've got to sneak into the East Wing and return the letter, I thought. *I don't want any evidence that I snuck in there earlier, especially if someone, or the ghost, is up there searching for it. And the sooner, the better. But . . . how? I can't get caught by the ghost . . . or anyone else for that matter. Not after nearly getting in trouble this afternoon.*

Then an idea struck me. *If I could get away from the party . . . even for just a few minutes, while everyone else is occupied . . .*

It was a ridiculous plan. I'd be the center of attention at my birthday party; how could I possibly sneak away without being noticed?

But there would never be a better time to return the letter to its rightful place.

I'll try, I vowed. *I'll try my best to get away and put the letter back where it belongs.*

"Miss Kate?"

I was so lost in my own thoughts at the moment

that Shannon's voice sounded very far away.

"Do you like it?"

I glanced at my reflection in the mirror. Behind me, Shannon stood nervously, waiting to see my reaction to the hairstyle she'd created.

"Oh, Shannon," I breathed. "It's beautiful." My hair flowed down my back as sleek and shiny as a waterfall. Loose wisps of hair framed each side of my face; other strands were fastened in the back with a clip made of rubies and onyx. Shannon had also woven dozens of tiny rubies through my hair, which sparkled whenever I moved my head.

"Now, let's get you dressed," Shannon said. "I swear I've been hearing motorcars coming and going for half an hour now."

My pulse quickened. "They're here? The guests are here?"

"A great many of them, I'd guess, from the sound of things," Shannon said. She held open my gown and steadied me as I stepped into it as carefully as I could. My beautiful birthday gown! I'd been dreaming of wearing it for weeks, and now the moment was here at last. It was made of crimson silk, with matching ribbons

to hold the mountains of ruffles in place, and there was a long row of glittering onyx buttons up the back. After she finished with the buttons, Shannon wrapped the velvet sash around my waist and tied it into a perfect bow. The sleeves were just slightly puffed and so light that they fluttered like butterfly wings whenever I moved. Next Shannon helped me with my elbow-length satin gloves and my shoes, delicate slippers that had been made in New York just for me. Finally, Shannon draped the Katherine necklace around my neck and fastened its clasp. I felt calmer, *stronger*, just from wearing it. And when I looked into the full-length mirror, I could hardly believe my appearance. Somehow, in the course of one afternoon, I seemed so much more grown-up—sophisticated, even. My eyes sparkled as brightly as my great-grandmother's, and when I smiled, it was Beth's grin I saw reflected back at me.

We walked toward the stairway in silence. Shannon was right; judging from the sounds—clinking glasses, strains of music, an endless hum of chatter—all the guests were waiting for me. I tried to take a deep breath, but it caught in my throat.

"You mustn't be nervous, Miss Kate," Shannon said, as though she could read my mind. "This is *your* moment, and you'll be absolutely brilliant. I know it. Your cousin felt the same way, you know; she was trembling like a leaf. But when she started her descent down the grand staircase . . . well, it was like a transformation. I think—if I might be so bold—the Chatswood blood that runs in your veins is always at the ready. Now, and whenever you need it most."

"Thank you, Shannon," I whispered, squeezing her hand. No wonder Beth was so fond of her.

"I'll see you afterward," Shannon promised me. "And if you need *anything* during the party, anything at all, I'll be right outside the ballroom, waiting for you."

"I know you will," I replied.

Then I turned away from Shannon.

And began my walk down the stairs.

The first thing I noticed as I reached the landing that led to the ballroom was that all the doors leading to the courtyard had been flung open; the walls were dripping with red roses; the cake, a creamy confection studded with cherries and perched on a wheeled cart, was taller than me. It was only after my eyes adjusted to the grandeur of it all that I saw the dazzle of the chandeliers, the enormous crowd of guests, and—much to my relief—the beaming faces of my family. I was even glad to see Alfie, and that's something I never thought I'd say!

A long receiving line formed at the bottom of the stairs, led by my parents, who covered me with kisses as they embraced me. Two distinguished men stood beside Mother.

"Kate, my dear, you surely remember Governor Pothier

and Mr. Gainer, mayor of Providence," Mother said by way of introduction.

"Happy birthday, Miss Vandermeer!" Governor Pothier announced as he bowed and kissed my hand.

"And many happy returns," added Mayor Gainer.

Then came Mr. Thomas Archimbauld, the president of the University of New England, Mr. Arthur Andrews, president of the United Coal Company, and Dr. Miriam Schofield, the only doctor that Great-Grandmother Katherine would permit to treat our family. And on and on and on until, finally, Alfie appeared before me.

"Happy birthday, Sis," he said with a sly grin.

I raised an eyebrow. "Frogs?"

"I sent them home," he confessed. "Their, uh, invitations were revoked."

Before I could think of a smart retort, Father whisked me onto the dance floor for the first dance of the evening. It began a whirlwind and continued that way, too—just as I'd suspected it would. I was grateful for the sandwiches Mrs. Taylor had sent to my room, for I scarcely had a chance to try any of the delicious food that Mrs. Hastings had prepared.

Midway through the evening, Father gestured for the orchestra to stop. "If I might have everyone's attention," he announced, "we request the pleasure of your company in the courtyard."

What's going on? I wondered.

Father led me over to the railing, where we stood together. I could hear the waves crashing on the beach down below. The rest of the family soon joined us. I noticed that all the servants were assembled in the back as well. It made me smile to see Shannon and Hank next to each other, so close that their shoulders touched. Whatever surprise my parents had planned must've been something special indeed.

First I heard a high-pitched whistle, followed by a *pop* and a *bang*. Everyone gasped at the explosion over the ocean—sparks like stars twinkling and tumbling into the waves. Then another, and another, and another.

Fireworks! I thought, beaming at the night sky. *My favorite!* I glanced around at all the shining faces around me—everyone with wide eyes, staring transfixed at the show.

That was when I realized: This was my moment to slip away unnoticed.

Go, I thought. *No one will even realize you're gone.*

But it wasn't easy to leave. The most glorious fireworks I'd ever seen were glittering right above my head, and almost every person I loved in the whole world was here to celebrate with me. I dearly wanted to stay.

Then I remembered how Beth had left her own twelfth birthday ball last month, in her attempts to clear Shannon's name. Did my cousin dawdle, dragging her feet in reluctance even though she knew the right thing to do?

No. She did not.

There will be other fireworks displays, I reminded myself. *But there will* never *be a better time to return the letter*. And I knew that that was the truth, even though I wished it weren't so.

I took the tiniest, most tentative step backward. People shifted a bit, making way without even looking at me. I felt a little giddy as I slipped through the crowd. It was going to work!

Vandermeer Manor had never stood so silent; I had to be the only one inside its walls. I ran all the way to my bedroom, where the letter and Nellie's keys were still hidden under my pillow. The feeling of aloneness

pressed in on me from all sides as I continued to the East Wing. With each step, my heart beat a little harder, hammering in my chest. I clenched the keys tightly so that my trembling fingers wouldn't make them jangle. *There are no such things as ghosts*, I repeated in my mind. *There are no such things as ghosts.* But no matter how many times I thought it, I couldn't forget the veiled figure I'd seen outside, sweeping through the mist. . . .

I forced myself to hurry through the silent, snaking halls. Finally, the door to the East Wing loomed before me. *Almost done now*, I thought. *Just open the door, replace the letter, and leave.*

But as soon as the door creaked open, a hiss filled my ears.

"Stay away."

I wasn't alone after all.

There was someone standing in the darkened hallway.

It's the ghost! I thought wildly as a cry of terror escaped from my throat. *She's here! She's waited for me!*

"Stay away."

My heart seized; I thought it might stop beating

altogether. I wanted to run away, run as far and as fast as I could. With the letter still clutched in my hand, I took a step backward, away from the door, away from the East Wing, away from that shadowy figure hovering in the gloom.

But at that moment, I remembered what Beth had said: *I've always thought you were the brave one.*

I forced myself to walk farther into the East Wing, though it took every ounce of courage I could muster.

"Stay away."

"Who are you?" I asked. My voice shook, but only a little.

A match was struck; a lamp was lit; and I found myself face-to-face with the stranger from the shadows. She was no ghost, but a very old woman—older even than Great-Grandmother Katherine—dressed entirely in black silk. She seemed as curious about me as I was about her. Just to see that she was a real flesh-and-blood person—and not some specter from beyond the grave—calmed my frantic heart.

"So you're the one who took the letter," she said. "I thought as much. As soon as I saw the picture had been disturbed, I told your great-grandmother—"

"You know my great-grandmother?"

Her wrinkled face broke into a smile. "Of course I know her. Your great-grandmother is the reason I'm here."

"But who are *you*?"

She tapped her chest. "I'm Essie. Essie Bridges."

Essie Bridges! The author of the journal—the lady's maid to young Katherine and Elizabeth! "H-how?" I stammered. "How did you—"

"Katherine begged me to come to America with her—oh, this was long ago, long before your time. She put on a brave face, and she was starry-eyed with love, but there was still a touch of fear in her. To leave her home and her people behind, especially her beloved sister, and to start a new life in a strange land . . . it was not an easy decision for her, or for me. It broke my heart to leave my other girl behind. But I couldn't very well let your great-grandmother face whatever the future would hold without a friendly face from home."

"So you came with her and Great-Grandfather Alfred," I said.

Essie nodded. "Yes, I served as her lady's maid

in America, just as I had in England. Then the sun-sickness came."

Far away, I could hear the explosions of the fireworks; we would've been able to see them from the window if the curtains hadn't been drawn so tightly.

"What sickness?" I asked.

"If it has a name, I'm sure I don't know it." Essie sighed. "But if I go into the sunlight, I get frightful rashes and blisters all over my skin. People see me and think I have the measles or the pox. But it's not catching. No one ever got sick from being near me. I swear it."

"Oh, Essie. I'm so sorry."

"So was your great-grandmother. No matter what she told everyone—the other servants, the people in town—they'd run away when they caught sight of me." Essie's voice broke as the memory brought tears to her eyes. "Out of the kindness of her heart, she hid me away here, and lo these many years *she's* been taking care of *me*. Can you imagine? The highborn daughter of a lord looking after a poor servant like myself. She brings me food, keeps me company, and most days she walks with me before sunrise so that I might take the

air. If I'd had a daughter of my own, she couldn't have cared for me better than your great-grandmother."

"I saw you!" I said suddenly. "I saw you walking—you were wearing a veil—"

Essie nodded. "Aye, that was me. I cover up just in case the sun rises earlier than I expect."

"But how do you get in and out without anyone ever seeing you?" I asked.

"Through an old servants' entrance to the East Wing, of course," Essie replied. "Might be you never noticed it downstairs; it's nearly grown over with ivy."

"So there was never any ghost?"

"Ghost? I should think not," Essie said. "Though your great-grandmother played no small part in spreading those stories—she had to keep everyone away from the East Wing somehow. And now it's been so many years that I don't think there's anyone downstairs who remembers old Essie. Of course, I know all about them; Katherine keeps me informed. The lady's maid and the chauffeur . . . now there's a tale for the ages."

"You know about Shannon and Hank?"

"I do. And I know how you helped them." Essie gave me a long look. "You certainly take after your

great-grandmother. The girls in this family will do anything for love."

"What do you mean?"

In the distance, I could still hear the fireworks going off. But there was one more thing I needed to ask Essie before I could return to the party. I held up the letter. Essie nodded.

"Thank you for returning this to me," said Essie. "I've been searching all over for it."

"You're welcome," I replied. "But why did you have it? It was written to my great-great-aunt Elizabeth."

"The answer to that question should best come from your great-grandmother," Essie replied.

Pop-pop-pop-pop-pop-bang-bang-bang-pop-pop-pop!

"The grand finale!" I gasped. "I've got to go! But . . . I'd like to come back sometime, if you wouldn't mind another visit from me—"

A smile spread across Essie's face. "Yes, Miss Kate, I think I'd like that very much."

I handed the letter to Essie and ran out the door as quickly as I could. The last sparks were falling into the ocean when I reached the courtyard, breathless

and disheveled. I glanced around anxiously, but no one seemed to be looking for me.

Then my eyes met Great-Grandmother Katherine's. She stood at the opposite end of the courtyard, watching me. She must've seen my madcap dash through the ballroom.

I've got to talk to her, I realized. *Tonight.* I wanted to talk to her about Essie . . . and about her mother's letter to Elizabeth.

It wasn't easy to get through the crowd as everyone made their way back inside. Suddenly, Alfie appeared before me. "Hey, Sis! Hold up."

"Not now, Alfie. I really have to—"

"But I haven't given you your birthday present yet."

He held out a big box tied with a red ribbon. I eyed it with suspicion. Who knew what lurked inside? Then I noticed the large air holes poked all over the box.

"Oh, no," I said. "No, no, no."

"Trust me, Kate. You're going to love it."

"I don't want one of your disgusting frogs, Alfie. No, thank you." I pushed the box back toward him . . . and heard the sweetest, faintest little *meow*.

My eyes grew wide. "Was that . . . ?"

Alfie grinned at me. "Told ya you'd love it."

I ripped off the ribbon and found a tiny orange-and-white kitten staring up at me with golden eyes. "Oh! Alfie! How did you—"

He scuffed his shoe along the ground. "I knew I couldn't compete with the Katherine necklace," he said. "But I thought little Scruffers here would be a fine runner-up."

"Scruffers? That's an awful name," I chided my brother, but my smile told him I was teasing. "Alfie, would you ask Shannon to bring the kitten to my room? I have to talk to . . ."

I trailed off. When I looked across the courtyard, my great-grandmother was gone.

I waited all evening, but Great-Grandmother Katherine never returned to the party. I knew I couldn't sneak away again—not when there were candles to blow out and cake to cut and waltzes to dance. It was nearly midnight when the last guests departed; I hardly dared to hope that my great-grandmother would still be awake. Her bedroom door was shut tightly, and I couldn't tell if her light was on. *I wish I could knock*, I thought as I hovered in the hallway. *But it would be wrong to wake her.*

"Miss Kate? Can I help you?" It was Gladys, carrying a cup of warm milk and four sugar cookies on a small plate.

My heart leaped. "Is my great-grandmother still awake?" I asked excitedly.

"Yes," she said. "Though not by choice. Sleep has proved elusive tonight."

That explains the milk, I thought. "Would you tell her that I'd like to speak with her?"

Gladys pursed her lips. "Miss Kate, she is *very* tired. Perhaps you can speak with her in the morning instead?"

I tried not to sigh. "Of course," I said. "Thank you, Gladys."

Back in my room, Shannon was playing with the kitten. "Miss Kate! What a darling birthday present."

"Isn't she sweet?" I asked as I sat on the floor.

"And pretty, too," Shannon said. "With ginger hair like your cousin."

I smiled; the kitten's fur did look a lot like Beth's hair. "Maybe I should call you Bethie," I said to the kitten.

"That's a fine idea," a new voice said.

Great-Grandmother Katherine was standing in the doorway!

"Gladys brought me too many cookies," she said. "Would you like some? Then we can both have sweet dreams tonight."

"Miss Kate, I'll fetch you some milk," Shannon said as she rose.

Great-Grandmother Katherine, all bundled in her dressing gown, crossed the room and sat on the edge of my bed. I climbed up next to her, cradling Bethie in my arms. Great-Grandmother Katherine placed her wrinkled hand on mine. "What a birthday, Kate! I hope you had a grand time."

I nodded. I'd had a wonderful birthday, although I was missing Beth desperately.

Great-Grandmother Katherine must have read my mind. "All day I've wanted to talk to you, Kate. I'm so sorry that Beth had to leave. It is never easy to say good-bye to someone you love."

"Yes," I whispered.

"But times are different now," she continued. "The ocean gets less and less difficult to cross. I have no doubt that you and Beth will see each other again—hopefully soon."

"I hope so," I replied.

"And heaven knows what you girls will get up to next time!" she said, chuckling. "It did me good to see you two cavorting about the house, whispering your secrets and concocting your plans. It reminded me of my dear sister and the sweet days

of our youth at Chatswood Manor."

"Great-Grandmother," I began. "I have to tell you something. I know about Essie."

She didn't blink. "Yes, I thought as much," she said. "Beth brought Essie's journal all the way from Chatswood, I suppose."

"How did you know?"

"The chant, of course—the one you girls did with your necklaces in the alcove." Great-Grandmother Katherine smiled. "I was visiting Essie in the East Wing, and we heard every word. There was only one way you could've known about it: from Essie's journal. I laughed, but she was horrified to think of Beth scurrying through Chatswood's secret passages."

My great-grandmother leaned forward. "Did you put the necklaces together?" she asked in an excited whisper. "Did you find the secret compartment?"

My smile faded. "Yes," I said slowly. "We did."

"And the puzzle? Were you able to solve it?"

"Apart forever."

A mysterious smile flickered across my great-grandmother's face. "No wonder the long face. That would be a sad phrase to find, wouldn't it?

"My sister and I wrote a message—more like a promise to each other, I should say—long ago when we were just girls still," she continued. "Then we cut it into tiny pieces and hid half of them in my necklace, and half of them in hers. That way, we would always carry the message close to our hearts."

She lifted the Katherine necklace and shook it close to my face. I strained my ears to listen. Then I heard the faint rustle of paper.

"Seems to me that some of the letters are still inside," she said. "And maybe some are still inside the Elizabeth necklace too."

"So what does the message really say?"

Great-Grandmother Katherine looked beyond me into the distance. "A part of you forever," she recited with one hand pressed to her chest.

I was so relieved that I started to laugh. "Oh, that's so much better!" I exclaimed. "And now I've *got* to see Beth again so that we can unlock the rest of the letters."

"I quite agree."

All this talk about letters made me remember the real reason why I wanted to speak with her. "I have to ask you something," I began. "As you know,

I discovered Essie's room this morning. I'm sorry. I didn't mean to snoop. I had no idea she was there, Great-Grandmother."

She smiled at me. "I suppose I'm grateful that my ruse about the ghost worked for as long as it did."

I pressed on. "I found the letter that your mother wrote to Elizabeth," I said. "But where is yours?"

Great-Grandmother Katherine closed her eyes. The moments passed and still she did not speak. The she leaned forward and took both my hands in hers. I sat up straight; for some reason, my heart had started pounding.

"Kate," she began. "I have something to tell you."

Every Secrets of the Manor book leads to another.

Read on for a first look at

Elizabeth's Story, 1848

I rolled over and stretched, enjoying the coziness of my silk down comforter. A housemaid had already been in to build up my fire, the gentle warmth it gave off welcome on these chilly June mornings. I could almost hear the house, Chatswood Manor, waking with me, ready to greet another day.

I knew that downstairs, servants were going about their morning routines, quietly bustling about, opening curtains, building fires, dusting, and cleaning. Our cook, Mrs. Fields, was no doubt scolding the kitchen maids to work more efficiently to whip eggs or slice bread for our breakfast, and Mr. Fellows, the butler, would be instructing the footmen on their tasks for the day before reading the newspaper and finishing his own breakfast in the servants' dining room. Mr. Fellows made a point of talking to Papa about the news of the day every morning when he served our meal in the family dining room.

Early morning was my favorite time of day. For a few moments every morning, when my mind was no longer asleep but not quite fully awake, I could almost forget that Mama had died just a few weeks ago.

But then, as always, I remembered. That now-familiar sinking feeling crept into my chest and settled in my heart. Next came the sting of tears behind my eyelids.

I sat up and reached for the silken bellpull that would call my lady's maid, Essie Bridges.

I promised myself that I would stop this, I thought, wiping my eyes. *And more important, I promised Katherine. We made a vow to be strong for each other, and for Papa.*

It was as if Katherine, my twin, could read my thoughts. At that moment, she walked through the dressing closet that connected our two bedchambers and leaned against the wall, a sleepy half smile on her face. Her eyes, too, had a trace of tears.

Katherine and I were so nearly identical that only Mama could tell us apart in an instant. The only obvious physical difference between us was in our hair:

Katherine's had a lovely natural wave while mine was stick straight. I envied Katherine that wave she had in our hair, while Katherine envied the fact that I was a half inch taller than she and five minutes older. I teased her that I would gladly give her my half inch in height if she would give me her wavy hair.

"I just heard Papa's valet in the hall instructing Mrs. Cosgrove to meet us in the library after breakfast. We're going to discuss the guest list for the birthday ball," Katherine said. "We'd better ring for Essie."

"I was just about to," I said, reaching again for the bellpull. The pull was connected to a bell in the servants' hall downstairs, where our ladies' maid, Essie, would hear it and come to our aid. Essie had been with Katherine and me since we were very young. We loved her dearly. It was Essie who helped to dry our tears after Mama died and Essie who always knew just what to say when we were feeling down or scared. She wasn't a blood relative, of course, but she was as much family to us as we were to each other.

I can still remember the first time Katherine and I met Essie. Essie has told me that I was too little to really remember all of these details, but I swear I do!

Katherine and I were puzzling over the alphabet in the nursery, trying to put our blocks in the correct order, when Essie came in, a bright smile on her pretty face. Immediately, I knew that she was different from all of the other servants I was used to seeing. There was something very special about her. She crouched down next to us and told us her name was Essie Bridges and that she was going to help take very good care of us. Then she attempted to help us with our letters, but as it turned out, she didn't know them either. Later, after Katherine and I were taught to read and write by our tutors, we taught what we had learned to Essie. She resisted at first, telling us it wasn't a good use of her time and that our parents weren't paying her to learn; they were paying her to care for us. But Katherine and I insisted! We kept after her until she relented. It didn't seem right to us that Essie couldn't enjoy reading books as we could. She was a quick study—I daresay she learned even more easily than Katherine and I had. But then again, perhaps she had better teachers!

While we waited for Essie this morning, Katherine plopped onto my bed to talk about our birthday, which was just over two weeks away. We had had parties before, of course, but for our twelfth birthday, Papa was throwing us a true birthday ball with more guests than we could count, a full orchestra, and beautiful custom-made dresses to wear. We had even been taking lessons with a dancing master.

This party was going to be the most spectacular social event of the season, perhaps even the year! In getting ready for the ball, it was as if Papa's estate, Chatswood Manor, and all of its inhabitants were shrugging off our sadness about Mama and beginning to live again.

"I can't wait to waltz with someone other than Mr. Wentworth," Katherine said.

We were giggling and whispering about dancing with boys when we heard a quiet knock on the door.

"Come in, Essie," I called.

"Good morning, Lady Elizabeth. Good morning, Lady Katherine," Essie said, walking quickly into the room and smiling at us as she did each and every morning. "What are you girls giggling about?" she asked us in a mock-serious voice.

"Nothing!" Katherine and I said in unison.

"Now, I'm quite sure I don't believe that!" Essie